# Different Stars

Jenn Faulk

ISBN:0989253805
ISBN-13:9780989253802

# DEDICATION

To Ana -- if your world travels lead you to Namibia, take me with you.
Love who you are becoming in Christ.

# CONTENTS

# ACKNOWLEDGMENTS

Thank you, again, to Wes for always being so supportive. Without your encouragement, I would still be writing stories and hiding them in a drawer somewhere. Who knew people would actually enjoy reading them, right? Mom, thanks for reading the rough draft of this story and saying that it was even better than the first book. Thank you to Swakopmund Baptist Church and all of the amazing friends I have an ocean away. My two years in Namibia were unforgettable, and I hope I've captured just a fraction of how incredible the "smile of Africa" is here in the pages of this book. And finally, a HUGE thank you to those who read Resolutions and wanted more. So thankful for you, and so excited to give this book to you...

# 1 CHAPTER ONE

I have a sense for big moments.

I get a feeling – part dread, part anticipation – when a big moment is about to unfold before me.  Call it a premonition, a hunch, or just a cautionary nudge from God, but whatever it is, this sensitivity for life changing moments has always been a part of who I am.

And just a week away from my thirtieth birthday, I sensed the biggest moment yet, as Bryan and Christy told me that they had incredible news.  For the mission board, for Costa Rica, and for me.

I had gone onto the foreign mission field to teach school, first and foremost.  I had been a kindergarten teacher back in the US, so I was well prepared to teach the twenty missionary children who fit into the age group there in Costa Rica when I was called to the position a year earlier.  The mission board's team was huge, and as I got to know the missionaries as I taught their children, I became involved in what they were doing and in how they were ministering to nationals.  My idea to begin using the local women's talents to make jewelry and beadwork, take those products back to the US, and sell them for a profit that went entirely back to the women, was one that took off immediately.  The goal was to help them earn income, alleviating poverty, all while introducing them to Christ through our witness as we worked alongside

3

them. Christy, the wife of our team leader, Bryan, and one of my best friends there in Costa Rica, took on the project alongside me, and we had our hands full the entire year.

I was happy. Happier than I had ever been in the US, and I was anticipating, after an upcoming, short trip back to Texas to build more interest in our project and raise support for what was being done, another two years of life changing ministry.

I was surprised, then, by the conversation in Bryan and Christy's small apartment just outside of San Juan.

"Sara," Bryan said kindly, bringing out an envelope as Christy sat down beside me, taking my hand in hers. "We've gotten a request from the mission board."

"A request?," I asked, as Christy squeezed my hand. "I hope it's good."

"Well," she said, tearing up. "Great for you and for the mission board." She looked sadly at her husband. "But not so much for us."

"How so?," I asked, concerned.

"We've just gotten word from headquarters. Sara, they're so impressed and so pleased with what you've done here. The center is just... well, it's beyond anything that they even envisioned when they appointed you to your teaching position."

I smiled. "I love the center. I love the ladies there. It's the best part of being here, honestly." I paused for a moment. "Is the board... are they wanting me to expand it?"

"Yes," Christy said. "That's it exactly. They want to expand the center."

"Oh!," I exclaimed. "I have some great contacts I'm already working with stateside, and we could arrange to have a team come out to put up another building. We could get work for at least fifty other women at first, of course, but there's no limit to what —"

"Sara," Bryan said softly. "The expansion isn't... isn't in Costa Rica."

And there it was – the sense that something big was about to happen. "It isn't... what?"

"They want you to do what you've done here," Christy said, "in another place. To create work for women in another place so that they can support themselves and come to Christ, just like they have here."

"Another place?," I asked. "Bryan, are they –"

"Sara, they're sending you to Africa. To a country called Namibia."


There was plenty to contemplate over the next week.

There was leaving Costa Rica and all that had been home for the past year. So many tears, so many hugs, and so many promises to keep in touch – it had been exhausting. Then, before I could even get my bearings back in the US, I was celebrating my thirtieth birthday. The age was one I had dreaded for a long time, assuming that being single and without the security of a husband and the promise of children in my near future as I said goodbye to my twenties would be heartbreaking. But as it was, I was so preoccupied with the transition from one side of the world to the next that it barely registered with me that I was now what I had always considered "old."

Besides, I certainly didn't feel thirty.

"And you don't look it either," Melissa said to me as we cut into the birthday cake she had brought to my parents' house.

"Not at all," Emily agreed with a smile. "You look amazing, Sara."

Melissa and Emily had always been my best friends. The three of us had grown up at Grace Community Church together, and through all the years, the miles, and the challenges afforded to us in our lifetime together, we had remained close, almost like sisters. The past year had been the most trying of all, with both Emily and Mel marrying and with me moving overseas. I had wondered a year ago, when we all said goodbye, if our friendship would weather the transitions, and I was so pleased to find that we had only grown closer. It was a treasure, having two friends who were so supportive, so loving, so encouraging –

"Sara looks great, but you look like death, Em," Melissa said, rather bluntly.

Emily studied her for a moment. "I feel like death, honestly."

"Should've gotten a flu shot," Mel shook the icing-covered knife in her direction. "Why you're so opposed to vaccinating yourself, I'll never know. Bet Sara got one."

"I sure did," I affirmed, taking a bite of the exquisite cake. "Along with every other shot known to modern science. Even had to get a rabies shot in preparation for Namibia."

"Insane," Mel said. "But at least if you bite someone, they're safe, right?"

I laughed at this, then glanced over at Emily, who was looking a little green around the edges, holding her hand to her mouth.

"I'm sorry you're sick," I said. "Maybe it's just a 24 hour bug, huh?"

She shook her head, managing a weak smile. "No, this one's a nine month bug."

We all three watched one another for an astonished moment.

Then, Melissa dropped the knife straight into the cake as I burst into happy tears, reaching out for Emily. "A baby!," I cried. "How far along are you?"

"Uh... ten weeks, I think," she sighed. "This one... isn't the first. We were pregnant this summer, then miscarried. I only knew I was expecting for two days."

"Em," Melissa said softly, "why didn't you tell me?"

Emily wiped away a few tears. "Josh and I were so sad," she explained. "We didn't want anyone else to have to feel like that with us. And he'd die if he knew I was telling you now, because we were going to wait to make sure that.... " She looked up at me, crying in earnest now. "But I don't care, because Sara's here and you're here, and I wanted to tell you *both*."

"I'm so glad you did," Melissa hugged her. "A baby! Don't let my mother-in-law hear about this."

"Trish wants you and Beau to have a baby, too?," I asked, wiping my eyes.

"Ugh, yes," Melissa rolled her eyes. "I have to keep my birth control pills under lock and key when we visit them for fear that she'll snoop around, find them, and replace them all with candy."

This made Emily laugh out loud as well.

"So," I asked softly. "Were you pregnant when you and Josh came to Costa Rica?" I bit my lip, worried that perhaps their visit to me, to help with some projects we'd been doing had compromised her pregnancy, and –

"I know what you're thinking," she answered, just as softly. "And that wasn't it. It wasn't anything like that. We weren't pregnant when we got there... we were when we left, even though I didn't know until later. But the trip? Had nothing to do with how it all ended up. I promise."

"I'm so sorry," I said.

"It's okay, honestly," she sighed. Then, with a smile, "Ironically enough, THIS baby was an overseas souvenir as well."

7

"The trip to Japan for your brother's wedding?," I asked.

Emily's brother, who was stationed in Okinawa with the Marines, had just very recently gotten married. The whole extended family had made the trip out together, and as Emily had emailed me, it had been a test of her patience and goodwill, as all the time spent in such close quarters, 24-7, with her mother and sister had been a real hardship.

"I thought you said you hardly got a moment alone with Josh the whole trip, what with everyone freaking out about the wedding," Melissa said.

"We managed at least a few minutes, obviously," Emily sighed. "I never even got to the point of feeling sick with the baby this summer, so even this? Throwing up all the time? Is wonderful. Just reassuring, you know?"

"Well, now, it's going to be even *harder* to leave," I whispered around my tears. "I want to see that sweet baby so badly."

"It'll just give you a reason to come back and visit," Emily smiled, holding my hands in her own.

"Most definitely," I said, hugging her again.

Namibia? Was far, far away.

I was beginning to feel every bit of my thirty years, plus thirty more, by the time my last flight landed in Windhoek, the capitol city. Still, though, I put on a smile, touched up my makeup, and prepared for a great welcome and introductions to a team that had remained mysteriously silent, with no communication towards me, in the time since I had heard that I would be joining them.

Emmanuel, a national worker for the mission, was the one to meet me outside of immigration. He was holding a sign up identifying himself as part of the Windhoek team, and I went over to him, expecting a warm reception, just as I had received from Bryan and Christy when I first arrived in Costa Rica nearly a year ago. Emmanuel, however, took one look at me, and his brow furrowed immediately.

"You do not look like Mr. Shiftoka," he said critically.

"Pardon? I don't look like… who?" I had just spent an incomprehensible number of hours on three separate flights. I was confused simply concerning what day and hour it was, but Mr. Shiftoka? This brought on a whole new kind of headache.

"Oh, Lord," Emmanuel breathed out, smiling and praying all at once. "I take it that… that *you* are the one sent from the mission?"

"Yes," I said, holding out my hand. "Sara Wright."

"Sarai," he said, laughing out loud. "Princess!"

I opened my mouth to ask what he meant, but he stopped me.

"I only mean to say that this name? It means Princess, right? In the Bible, Abram and Sarai, the mother of princes… a princess, yes?"

I sighed. "Well, I suppose so. Yes."

"Oh, Brother Daniel will be so pleased," Emmanuel laughed to himself again, taking my suitcases up in his arms and leading the way outside.

"Is… Brother Daniel… well, is he the man in charge? Of the team, I mean," I asked, hustling to keep up with Emmanuel's long strides as we crossed the porch towards the small parking lot.

"Brother Daniel *is* the team. The only missionary in all the country, as it is," Emmanuel said, just as the hot, dry air swirled around us and took my breath away. Seeing my shock at the arid surprise, Emmanuel smiled again. "This is east wind, Princess."

"Sara," I interrupted, losing patience with this enigmatic man.

"Sara, yes," he shook his head. Then again, "Brother Daniel will be so pleased."

"What's east wind?," I asked, even as the sand began to bite at my legs uncomfortably.

"It is life here, unfortunately," he said, throwing my suitcases roughly into the back of a small truck. "The wind from the veld and dunes sweeps through the whole of Namibia, you see? And it's hot. Unbearably, cruelly hot, in the middle of the winter. It is much worse on the coast. Much, much worse in Swakopmund."

"Swakopmund?," I asked. "That's where I'm going, isn't –"

"Is it?," Emmanuel laughed out loud. "Swakopmund! Brother Daniel will be *so* pleased. Get in the bakkie, Princess – we shall go and show him just what the mission board has sent to him."


Brother Daniel was... well, he was a jerk.

Emmanuel had driven me straight through Windhoek, pointing out landmarks and pleasantly detailing some of the city's history as we drove, looking at me doubtfully but not rudely as we approached the gates for the mission property. "It is an amazing country, this Namibia is," he said, as he jumped out of the bakkie, throwing over his shoulder, "it is a shame you will not get to know it better."

Before I could correct him, he was jogging to the gate, calling to a boy sitting guard outside in a language I didn't recognize. Then, he was back in, driving through as the boy held the gate open and stared at me openly.

"Such a surprise, such a surprise," Emmanuel said almost gleefully.

As soon as we stopped, he was out again, running to the back to get my suitcases, then looking at me. "We best leave them here, Miss Sara," he said. "Until we figure out what Brother Daniel will do."

"Until we figure out what Brother Daniel will do?," I said, rather irritated. "I'm here to do a job, with my own orders to follow, and—"

He looked alarmed. "I did not mean to offend you," he said. "It's just… well, we were expecting Mr. Shiftoka."

"Yes, you keep saying this. Who is Mr. Shiftoka?!," I practically shouted at him.

"Come," he said, shrugging his shoulders. "We will talk to Brother Daniel."

The mission was laid out very simply. Stucco, one floor buildings – one the size of an apartment, another the size of a garage, and a third the size of a closet – were contained within a security gate. There were two older looking trucks (or bakkies, as Emmanuel called them, pointing them out to me), and of all things, a basketball goal.

"I suppose Brother Daniel likes to shoot hoops?," I asked as we made our way to the smallest building.

Emmanuel looked at me, confused. "What? That? Well, you would think, but Brother Daniel? He doesn't do much besides work."

"Sounds like a fun guy," I muttered, but he didn't seem to hear me as he opened the door, shouting out with great delight, "Brother Daniel! I have your new missionary!"

I peered around Emmanuel's dramatically splayed arms to see a very attractive, very irritated, young American man, sitting behind a desk, a phone to his ear. He took one look at me, rolled his eyes, and shouted into the phone, "This is *unacceptable!*"


Thirty minutes later, Emmanuel shook his head at me sympathetically yet still with a great smile on his face, as he served me tea. I had endured half an hour of glares from the inhospitable Brother Daniel, who never hung up the phone but continued to go over, in exhaustive detail, his grievances with the mission board stateside.

The listening had informed me of many things – that I was *not* Mr. Abed Shiftoka, a Namibian national who was still in the US at this point, studying at a university and *not* coming back home to assist Daniel in the unreached parts of the country as he had been commissioned by the board to do. That had been the plan – for him to go study stateside, earn his degree, then come back to assist with language in the far reaches of the country – but Abed's plans had changed. Apparently. And Daniel hadn't gotten the memo until approximately thirty minutes before my plane landed, when the mission board called to inform him that instead, he was getting a missionary from the field in South America, sent to work with women in the DRC, a refugee camp at Swakopmund.

"Swakopmund?!," he continued shouting at the phone as I sipped my tea, wincing at the unexpected sweetness, then sipping it up almost greedily. It was like candy. "Why are we wasting personnel dollars for a holiday at the beach?!"

"It is Rooibos," Emmanuel whispered to me.

"What is?," I asked. "The beach?"

"No, no, no," he said, laughing at me quietly. "Rooibos. It's the tea. That's what it's called."

"Well, it's just great," I whispered back to him, "and I –"

"*Fine*," Daniel shouted. "Whatever. We'll deal with it." He hung up the phone abruptly, causing Emmanuel and me to stare at him.

I put my teacup down and waited for this monster of a man to finally speak *to* me instead of just *about* me.

"Who are you?," he said, sitting back and crossing his arms over his chest.

"Sara Wright," I said evenly. "I thought you were expecting me."

He sighed. "Well, I was expecting a man. A Namibian man. Who, you know, can speak Afrikaans. And German. And Oshiwambo. And Herero. Can *you* speak any of those?"

"I can speak Spanish," I said.

Emmanuel laughed out loud at this and pointed a finger at Daniel. "You see, they've sent you a *woman*. Who speaks *Spanish*." He raised his eyebrows at Daniel. "Someone, somewhere is having a very good laugh."

"Well, it's not here," Daniel said, continuing to glare at me. I mentally retracted my first thought regarding his attractiveness. With the scowl on his hot-tempered face, he was about as unattractive as any man I had ever seen.

We sat in silence for a moment.

"So... Sara Wright." He continued to glare. "Can you tell me what you were sent here to do?"

I held up my wrist, where I wore one of the beaded bracelets my ladies in Costa Rica had made. "Jewelry."

"Jewelry?," Daniel asked with no small amount of derision. Even Emmanuel stopped what he was doing to look at me oddly.

"I'm here to set up a center for women where they can make goods to sell. You know, make a sustainable income and all to support themselves."

Emmanuel nodded as though he thought this was a great idea, but his enthusiasm was cut short by Daniel's words. "Jewelry? You're going to take women who are starving, who have to watch their children die in the streets, and teach them how to make jewelry for rich, white American women?"

"Teaching them a skill will keep them from starving," I began. "I've seen it before, in Costa –"

"You haven't seen anything," he said, harshly. "You haven't seen this place."

I kept my mouth shut, holding in the harsh words that I so desperately wanted to say.

"Emmanuel," Daniel said, a mocking smile coming to his face, "I've been told by the mission board that Miss Wright is staying with us whether I want her to or not. And that we're to take her immediately to Swakopmund and make arrangements for her to stay." He looked at me. "Swakopmund... it's a holiday destination, you know. So, you'll really be suffering for the Lord and all. Going out to the DRC to help the starving women and all, then heading back to your flat to enjoy lobster."

Emmanuel looked at him, sensing that I was being pushed too far. Perhaps Daniel would have felt some remorse as well, had I not looked him straight in the eye and said, "I prefer steak, actually."

There was a moment of stunned silence. Emmanuel looked from me to Daniel, then back again. Then, he seemed to want to disappear entirely as Daniel slammed his hands down on his desk, causing me to jump in my seat.

"Well, then," he hissed at me with a tight smile. "Best be getting out there, huh?" He stood and began stuffing papers in a bag. "Emmanuel, I'm taking Miss Wright to the coast in... the next ten minutes," he said, glancing at his watch. "We'll be visiting the DRC, if you can get some supplies ready for me to take out there."

"Okay," Emmanuel said, heading outside to get the truck ready.

14

I tried reasoning with him. "But I can't pick up the keys on the flat I'm leasing until tomorrow –"

"Should have thought of that before you came all this way, I guess," Daniel said, his back still turned to me. "You can camp in the river bed."

"Are you being serious?," I gasped.

He looked me straight in the eye. "You want to see what it's like? What Namibia is *really* like? Well, we will."

I blinked at him. How very different this was from my welcome to Costa Rica, where Bryan and Christy met me at the airport, showed me around the city, had me stay with them for a few days before settling me into my new place with kind, supportive words –

"Emmanuel should have everything ready by now," Daniel cut into my thoughts.

"Fine," I managed. "My bags are still in the truck."


The first Namibian people I met were starving.

After a very silent drive across the country, where I fought the jet lag in an effort to see where I was going and where he was taking me, Daniel and I arrived in Swakopmund. Even as the ocean and the quaint, colorful buildings were coming into view, he took a detour up through the townships, pointing them out, naming them by names, and finally parking in a squatter camp far out on the edge of town.

"This is the DRC," he had said without any fanfare, as thin, hungry people surrounded the truck on all sides.

Daniel had jumped out, shouting out a greeting in a language I didn't recognize, as several people began crowding around him. I got out and numbly came to his side, where I felt my skirt being tugged in several different places. I looked down to see five small children, all of them covered in dust, flies buzzing around their faces, their hands held open towards me, saying words I couldn't understand.

"Um... Brother... Brother Daniel, I... what are they saying?" I looked at him helplessly.

"They want to know if you brought food," he said. "Because you're white. And white people must always have food."

"Well," I looked at him. "Do we? "

"We have some," he said, a flicker of compassion in his cold eyes, "but not enough. That's not the most pressing issue right now, though, according to these ladies," he gestured towards the few ladies who now clutched his arm, pulling him from me, even as one of them cried. "Can you grab my bag out of the bakkie?"

I did as he asked, even as he continued chatting in soothing, foreign tones with the women who led him away, and I rushed to follow them, more children coming up to me as I did so. As we neared one of the makeshift shelters – made mostly of garbage, it seemed – a horrific smell wafted up and hit me in the face.

"Oh, God," I managed.

"Yes," Daniel said. "By all means, start praying."

Inside the inadequate shelter was a child, lying on the dirt. His little stomach was puffed up, his hair was nearly white, and he wasn't moving. A man sat near him, stoically watching, as an elderly woman kept tending to the child, rubbing his face tenderly and cooing to him. When the pair saw Daniel, they stood to their feet, grasped his hand, and began very nearly shouting their concerns to him.

"Ja, ja," Daniel said calmly, kindly, patting them on the backs, then kneeling next to the unresponsive child. "Miss Wright –"

"It's Sara," I managed.

"Sara, then," he said, irritation back in his voice, "can you get the medical kit out of my bag?"

I began digging through the bag until I found it, handing it to him as I knelt across from him. "Are you a doctor?"

"Nope," he said confidently, even as he pulled a syringe from the kit and began looking for a vein on the small child.

"Then, should you be –"

"What choice do we have? I don't suppose you have a medical degree, do you?"

"I'm a kindergarten teacher," I gasped, shocked as he injected the dying child with who knows what.

"Well, that's helpful," he muttered. He rubbed his thumb along the child's face and spoke a few words to the crowd that had gathered. Then, placing his hand on the boy's chest, he bowed his head and prayed words I couldn't understand in a defeated tone that needed no translation.

Before I could properly gather myself back up, he was back out into the sun, as more and more people crowded around us with their worries and concerns.

"His father has AIDS," Daniel said by way of explanation, as if anything could explain the horror I had just witnessed. "His mother likely died from it. And he's the unlucky recipient of it as well. Which, you know, might not mean a death sentence anywhere else, but here? He's got parasites from the drinking water, he hasn't had a decent meal in months, and he probably has TB. I gave him something for the fever, so that he'll hopefully have a few last lucid moments."

My eyes filled with tears. "That's… that's horrible."

"That's reality," he said, glaring at me.

"I saw that you had some food in your bag," I told him, looking around at the crowd of children that wouldn't let me go. "Can we… can we at least leave it with them?"

"Sure," Daniel said, tossing me the bag. "You go right ahead."

I opened it to hand out what little we had, and as I held out just the first piece of fruit, tiny, hungry hands began clawing at me, at the bag, to get inside. I let out a gasp, shocked by their frantic reaching and pushing, as they all but ripped apart Daniel's bag until it was completely empty.

And then, they pushed up against me, even more closely, their cries and yells for more even louder than they had been ten seconds ago.

The images from the dying boy's home and this frantic, starving crowd raced through my mind even as I clutched the side of the bakkie weakly, unable to keep them from coming, even as I closed my eyes and prayed that I could forget, even for a little while, even as I was being pulled in several different directions.

Before I could do anything to stop myself, I leaned over beside the bakkie and threw up, gagging even as there was nothing left in my stomach. The smells and the sounds, the sights and the taste of sand and filth in my mouth brought tears to my eyes. Tears that were already pooled and ready to fall as I took in the devastation around me.

"Get in the bakkie," Daniel said, and I did so, hating him all the while.

He got in the driver's seat, slamming the door behind him, and accelerated as the sea of people surrounding us parted to get out of his way. He didn't even look my direction as he sped out of the DRC and into Mondessa, the township that was significantly better but so far removed from what I had ever considered enough. I couldn't stop sobbing.

"Are you done?," Daniel asked evenly.

"Why do you *hate* me?!," I yelled at him, finally done with his attitude.

"Are you actually crying because you think I hate you?" He glanced at me.

"No," I said, "I'm crying because there are children starving back there, and the man sent here to *help* them is so angry and bitter and cynical that he is *useless*."

Daniel looked as though I had slapped him. He seemed to be without words.

"I think," I said, "that I would do better on my own –"

"Let me tell you something," he said, finding his voice again. "Women out here? On their own? Namibian women? Are attacked every day. Raped. Beaten. And all but murdered. And they do need help, you're right, to keep from starving, to keep their children from starving. And what does the board do? They send me a *woman*. To come and teach a skill that isn't sustainable out here and certainly not with women who are so sick and frail that they can do *nothing* to protect themselves and their children. A woman who is so naïve and innocent as to what this place is *really* like that she'll be robbed blind just at the point where she's gotten others to put their trust in her. And so, everyone will be – pardon my language – royally screwed."

I continued wiping tears away, wishing myself as far away from him and this horrible place as possible.

"You can't teach people anything if you can't keep them alive, Sara. And I certainly can't do anything of any significance in being the hands and feet of Christ out here without some help. But you? You're not who I need because instead of alleviating the problem, you make it *worse*. You bring in your American, money-making plans without knowing *anything* about the people here. And added to that, now, instead of worrying about all of these national women living here, I also have to worry about the blond, beautiful, American woman I'm sending out there every day. Who, sad to say, can't even spend ten minutes out there without throwing up and crying."

I scowled at him. "It was the first time. It won't always be this hard, and I—"

"It will *always* be that hard," he said. "I've been here ten years, and it *never* gets easier. Seeing that, witnessing that, and knowing that there isn't a whole lot you can do for people beyond offering them hope for what comes *after* the disease and the hunger kills them. That's all you can do."

"I'm not stupid, you know," I whispered. "And I'm not worthless. Surely there's something I can do here to help."

He took another frustrated breath. "I didn't say you were stupid or worthless. I just –"

"You just can't see how anyone could do anything here, for people, for Christ, unless they're *you*," I spat at him. "Oh, I get it, Daniel. And I get why you're the *only* person out here. Because I can't imagine that *anyone* would want to work with a jerk like you. I know I don't."

We drove in silence for a while, the holiday town slipping past us as we went. By the time he pulled up to the beach, I had my backpack on and was ready to jump out as soon as he stopped the truck. "I can handle myself," I told him. "Go back to Windhoek."

I went around to the back to get my two suitcases... and stopped short when I saw that they weren't there. I was certain that they hadn't been left in Windhoek, and I had seen them when we got out at the DRC, and –

"What?," Daniel muttered, getting out of the truck. "What's –"

He stopped short at my expression.

"My things..." I said, weakly. "They're... gone."

"Oh, geez," he rolled his eyes. "Did you just *leave* them in the back of the truck when we got out?"

"What was I supposed to do?"

He looked at me like I was an idiot. "Lock them up in the cab of the truck! Lock up everything! I can't believe I even have to tell you that!"

I couldn't stop the tears from returning. "Those two suitcases were... all I had in the world, actually. Everything. Just gone."

Daniel blew out an exasperated breath, running his hands through his hair, no doubt considering the very few options the board had left him in sending out a clueless, naïve missionary to this place, and –

"It's okay," I said, in my bravest voice. "Whoever took them really needed all of that stuff more than I did. How can I even be upset when those children are dying out there, and the worst I have to deal with is... only having the clothes on my back, right?"

Daniel looked at me, a glimmer of sympathy on his face. Then, it was gone as another thought hit him. "Please tell me that you still have your passport."

"Oh, yeah," I said, relieved at this, at least, holding up my backpack for him to see. "Passport, lease, all of my documents, my laptop, and, hey! A change of clothes!" I smiled weakly. "See? It's good news after all. I'm just fine!" And I burst into tears again.

Daniel stared at me for a moment. No words of comfort, no move to help, nothing. Just staring with his intense, hateful, glaring way of doing everything, and –

"Like I said, just go to Windhoek," I said, turning away from him. "I'll be fine on my own."

# 2 CHAPTER TWO

I contemplated my options as I spent a restless night tossing and turning in the hotel room I arranged for myself without any concern as to what Daniel was going to do. A big part of me wanted to book the first flight back to Costa Rica, or failing that, to Texas, where I could forget this hateful man and this sad place. Then, part of me wanted to stay and dreaded to do so at the same time, thinking of the crime, the dangers, and the desolation and heartbreak of the DRC, knowing that surely something could be done and fearing that I would be the one to have to do it all at the same time.

But the most pressing desire I had that night, as I thought through my options, was to make a difference for Christ in the lives of so many hopeless, lost people living here. There wasn't much I knew about ministry or missions either one, honestly, but I knew Jesus and knew that He was worth living for, even here. I was making plans as I wrestled with my thoughts, coming up with a strategy, and seeing it all come together in my mind, as I finally drifted off to sleep.

The next morning, I knew what I had to do first. I showered, dressed, and arranged all my documents, double checking my Swakopmund map for the realtor's office. I was going to get my keys, get settled in, get acquainted with the national churches, ask for their help and assistance with the big plans I was making, and –

And there was Daniel, sitting on the seawall, right outside the hotel lobby. He looked up at me as I came out, his sunglasses hiding his eyes from me.

"What are you doing here?," I asked, hitching my backpack up onto my shoulders. "And how did you even know where I was?"

"Small town, beautiful blond American woman – wasn't hard to ask around and figure it out. And I'm here because I'm taking you to breakfast," he said, standing and brushing the sand off of his shorts.

"I don't want to go to breakfast with you," I said.

"Well," he sighed. "I probably deserve that." A pause. "Look. I'm sorry. You're right. I'm a jerk. And I certainly don't want you here –"

"Saying that isn't really helping your case about being sorry and all –"

He held up his hand. "My apologies. Again. But, like I was going to say, it doesn't matter what I want because you're here, and if you're here, then God must have a good reason for sending you here. So."

"So?" I looked at him. He was horrible. At everything. And apologies topped the list.

"So, are you going to let me take you to breakfast so we can figure out what in the world you're going to do here?," he spat out, exasperated as well.

"Fine. Whatever."


Three hours later, sitting outside at the little café where we'd just finished breakfast, he was only partially convinced that what I had

23

planned would work.

"I apologize for taking you to the DRC without any warning," he said, haltingly. "My intent was to scare you away."

"Noooo," I said around my coffee cup, in mock shock.

"Okay, so it didn't work," he said with a small smile. Then, all amusement was gone. "But I wanted you to see what it's like – what you're up against. I appreciate that you didn't just run away screaming. And that you didn't pass out when I stuck that kid."

"No, I didn't," I managed. "I did spend the rest of the night crying, however."

"Again, that was likely my fault," he said, sighing.

"Only partially," I said softly. Then, hesitating, "I didn't expect it to be... to be so sad."

"They're displaced people," he said. "They have no place at home anymore, and here? Well, it's better here than where they came from."

"It's hard to imagine that the DRC is better than anything."

"Yeah, I know," he said. "The best thing for you to do here at the beginning is to find nationals who care. Believers already here who know the language, understand the culture, and who have a heart to get out there and do the work with you."

I nodded. "Where should I begin? Do you know anyone? Any place I can start?"

He shrugged. "No clue, beyond the few pastors I know here. Swakopmund? Not really on my radar. What with it being a holiday town and all." He gave me a tight smile that held no joy at all.

"Well, then," I said, "it's going to be a tough job here at first."

"You would think," he said. "But I'm sure there will be a whole horde of young Afrikaner men lined up around the block just hoping and praying that there's some way they can help you out."

I heard the implication in what he said. I gave him an even look and a tight smile. "Well, let's hope so, Brother Daniel. Wouldn't that be fun?"

I was trying to count my money as the young Afrikaner man behind me stared in my direction.

I had my keys, had exchanged some of my American dollars, and was attempting to buy a loaf of bread and a jar of peanut butter. Real survival food, until I could rent a fridge.

Standing in line trying to figure it out, though, I began to wish that I had asked Daniel, even with all of his arrogance and rudeness, to come with me until I could figure out what I was doing. We had said goodbye an hour ago, and he had gone, with a copy of my lease in hand, to complete a whole list of tasks that needed to get done. I had been glad for a reprieve from his intense stares and exasperated expressions, but...

I needed his help figuring this out. The money was so colorful... and so confusing. What did the girl checking my groceries say? How much?

"Shame, man," the young man behind me finally said. "Do you know what you're doing?"

I bit my lip. "I... well, no." I looked at him with a smile. "New to... well, to here. What coin is this?"

"That's ten rand... dollars," he said. He exchanged a few words with the checker, then laughed. "What you need is the five coin. It's gold. Or if you have the ten note –"

"Like this?" I held up a blue bill.

"Ja, that's it."

I gave it to the cashier and got back a collection of coins.

"And there," the young man leaned over and pointed, "is the five coin. So you'll know next time."

"Thank you," I said, smiling at him. "I mean… baie dankie." The only Afrikaans phrase I knew.

He nodded, smiling back, "Pleasure."

"Riaan, het jy—"

The lovely young woman walking our direction stopped short at his side when she saw me. "Oh… goeie middag!," she said with a huge smile.

"Hi," I smiled back.

"Ag, man!," she screeched when she heard my accent. "Are you an American?"

The young man sighed and rolled his eyes, prompting her to hit his shoulder playfully.

"Just because *you* work with them all the time doesn't mean I *ever* get to meet one," she said, poking him in the chest. Then to me, "Are you one of Riaan's clients?"

I looked at her, confused. "One of who's what's?"

She laughed out loud. "Oh, I love the way you talk!"

I loved the way she talked even more, especially since each word was accompanied by such bright laughter in her sparkling eyes. She held her hand out to me, "I'm Ana Marie. And this is Riaan, my husband, and you are not one of the tourists he has been flying around then, hmm?"

"Flying around?," I asked, while gathering up my bags.

26

"He's a pilot – takes tourists into the bush and all. Owamboland, all that. Not you, though?"

I shook my head. "Well, I'm not a tourist, actually. I just moved to town. My name is Sara."

"Sara! I should like very much to talk with you about America sometime. We want to go there one day, see the sights and all, you know."

I smiled at her as the three of us made our way into the sunshine outside. "We'll have to talk then. I can give you some tips and pointers."

"Lovey," Riaan said to Ana Marie, smiling in my direction, "we should probably hold off on asking *her* questions about America until we've answered *her* questions about Namibia. Since, you know, we're all here right now, she's new, we're not, and –"

"Ja! How silly of me!," she laughed out loud. "We know *all* about Swakopmund. And Namibia. And... well, that's it, actually."

I laughed with her. "I would appreciate getting to visit with you then."

"Would you like to meet us for dinner tonight?"

"I would love that, Ana Marie," I smiled at her.

I was still smiling a few hours later, thinking on my conversation with these new friends. The Bothas. "Very Afrikaans last name," Ana Marie had said to me, then with lowered voice, "but Riaan has an English mother, you know. Not that I hold it against him, of course." I had tried to comment on this, but as she had for most of our walk back towards the sea, she went on with another topic, pointing things out to me and arranging to meet me later, giving me a huge hug as we said goodbye. What a warm welcome, so unlike Daniel...

… who even now, as I sat on the seawall, approached me with an irritated look on his face.

"Okay," he said without so much as a hello. "I have your passport, your visa, a copy of your lease, your receipt of deposit for the water company, the electric company, and internet provider, *and…*" with a flourish, "… your new phone."

"Thank you," I said, taking it from him and clicking through the contacts. "Daniel Boyd. Daniel Boyd. Daniel Boyd." I looked up at him. "Why are you in here three times?"

"Cell number, office in Windhoek, and the mission house in Oshakati. None of the other houses have phone service." He looked at me appraisingly. "What have you gotten done?"

"Well," I said, "I picked up my keys and bought a few groceries."

He looked at me, tilting his head to the side.

"Is that it?"

"Oh, and I switched my money over to *rand.*"

"They're dollars. Namibian dollars."

"Oh, no, they're rand, too. My friend, Riaan, told me."

His brow furrowed. "Riaan?"

I regarded him with just a little bit of the same pompous attitude he was always giving me. "Yeah, just one of those Afrikaner men you said would be lined up around the block to help out poor, stupid Sara, you know. I'm even meeting him for dinner."

"Wait a minute," he began. "First of all, I never said you were stupid, and –"

"You implied it, though, but I'm getting by just fine after all, huh?"

He was getting irritated with me. More so than usual. "And second of all, you don't need to be meeting up with random men and –"

"I'm meeting up with Riaan and his WIFE, Daniel."

"How do you already have dinner plans and friends after only three hours on your own?"

"Most people like me, you know," I huffed at him. "I'm a really likeable person!"

"Yes, I can tell with the way you're screeching at me like that," he frowned at me.

I looked at him thoughtfully. "I think we've gotten off on the wrong foot, you and me."

He didn't say anything to me for a moment. "And?"

"And," I said, irritated, "it might be nice if we were on better speaking terms since, you know, you're the only other person on this ridiculous 'team' AND since your number is the only one in my phone, right?" I rummaged around in my backpack, pulling out a slip of paper. "Shame, man," I said, adding a new contact from the slip of paper Ana Marie had given me, "you're not the only one now. B-O-T-H-A. There you go." I switched off the phone and looked at him.

"Shame, man?," he repeated, staring at me dubiously.

"It's growing on me, the way they talk," I said, allowing myself a smile.

He shook his head at me. "Okay, well, whatever. It sure seems like you're going to be… well, okay, I guess."

"Thank you for that vote of confidence."

"I need to get back to Windhoek this afternoon… so…"

"So… see you." I waved at him. I had very nearly had enough of him and his pointed glares, and –

He handed me his keys. I looked at them, confused, and chanced a glance back up at him. "What are these for?"

"The truck," he said, already irritated with me. Again.

"Aren't you going to need these?"

"I'm leaving the truck with you," he said. "I can hitch a ride back to Windhoek. Which, by the way, is something *you* should *never* do. And you'll have no need to since you'll have something to drive yourself now, obviously."

"You're leaving me… your truck?," I asked, surprised by his generosity, and –

"Mission board rules for the country. All personnel are required to have vehicles. There are two more back at the mission house."

Ahh. So much for generosity.

"Wait a minute… is it… an automatic?"

"No."

My heart dropped just a tiny bit. "Oh, Daniel. I…"

"Oh, geez," he muttered, running his hand over his face. "Please tell me you can drive a standard."

I shook my head pitifully, feeling more inept than I had ever felt before… which was really saying something in this strange new place.

"Fine," Daniel nearly shouted. "Guess we'll need to have a driving lesson before I head back to Windhoek then, huh?"

"And you're going to be such a patient teacher," I murmured. "I can already tell."

Two hours later, Daniel and I were barely speaking to one another. Oh, we had said plenty all over Swakopmund, as the truck died on me nearly every time I hit the brakes. Daniel couldn't fathom, as he explained in exhaustive detail, how a woman could have a college degree and appear to have her wits about her and still just *not get* how this relatively simple task of driving was supposed to work. I was very nearly ready to push him right out of the truck when he declared that he was satisfied enough by my skills and told me to drop him off at the edge of town.

"That was fun," he said sarcastically, jumping out and grabbing his stuff.

"Oh, well, you're a *fun* guy," I said through clenched teeth.

He shut the door behind him and leaned on the windowsill, looking at me thoughtfully for a moment.

"What?," I spat out at him.

"Are you going to be okay here? By yourself?"

"I'll be just fine," I said, giving him a tight, insincere smile.

"Call me when you get ready to run away screaming, okay?" He allowed himself a small grin, no doubt anticipating this day already, just so he could tell the mission board that he told them so.

Well, I'd show him. As he strolled away, I started the truck, intent on peeling out and leaving him in my dust, only to have it die on me as soon as I stepped off the clutch.

"Ugggghhh," I groaned, even as Daniel turned back around, shook his head at me, and kept on walking.

Welcome home, Sara.

"Why did you come here?"

Ana Marie had hardly touched her fish and chips. The Bothas and I sat along the seawall, our takeout in our laps, after an impromptu tour of the town. I had asked many questions, Ana Marie had answered even more than I had asked, but the greatest question hadn't occurred to her until that very moment.

"I'm a missionary."

Riaan's expression changed from congenial to hard, and Ana Marie, bless her heart, burst out laughing. "Seriously?"

"Seriously," I managed, around my food.

She continued studying me. "Like... a missionary? Like church and God and all of that?"

"Like... well, yeah." I smiled. "I'm going to start a project in the DRC."

This prompted all out stares from both of them. "Why?," Riaan managed after a moment of shocked silence.

"Well," I began, with a sigh, "Jesus taught that we were to care for those who were suffering, and I've only been there once, but... children are suffering there. Women, men... life is hard. I have some ideas about small business ventures, working with churches back in the United States, to create sustainable incomes for some of the women so that they can support themselves and their families and... well, not die in the DRC."

Riaan seemed to think about this for a moment, then nodded at me appreciatively.

Ana Marie, however, had only this to say. "You are *crazy*! The DRC? Riaan," she nudged her husband. "Our American friend is completely crazy."

I shrugged at her. I had heard it more recently than she would believe.

"Crazy… but I like that about you." She smiled at me. "Oh, Sara! Look, it's Swakopmund's finest – the sunset. The best part of being here."

And together, the three of us watched the sun fall off into the horizon, dipping below the Atlantic, as far out as we could see.

My parents had arranged to Skype with me that next morning. Early morning for me, late evening for them, but we coordinated and were ready.

"Sara?," Mom smiled at me gleefully.

"Hey, Mom," I said, smiling back at her. "Where's Dad?"

"Right here," he said, squeezing into the frame as well.

"I'm glad to see you guys," I sighed. "It's been the craziest couple of days here."

"We're glad to see you, too," my mother said, missing my last statement entirely, thanks to her preoccupation with something just beyond the edge of my screen. "As is someone else, who just happened to drop by tonight."

"Hey, Sara," he said, right before he came back into view.

Like I said, I have a sense for big moments. And I could feel that this was one, even as I heard him. I felt my breath catch at the all too familiar voice, only to have the reality of the situation confirmed as my eyes met his, half a world away.

"Jon?"

Jon and I had been together a long time.

I met him during our last year of college, and it was love. Crazy, sappy, stupid love.

For me, at least. From the first day I sat next to him in that stupid requisite health class that I had neglected to take my first seven semesters, I was infatuated with him. It wasn't that he was particularly handsome or particularly smart or even particularly charming.

I was just particular for him.

I had never had trouble catching anyone's attention before, even though I had never really tried. For as long as I could remember, I had been looking for something more serious than the casual, brief relationships that the guys who noticed me always seemed to be interested in having. By the time I met Jon, I had stopped giving most of them more than a look.

Maybe that was what was so appealing about him. There he was – not even looking my direction. He had put the class off until the last semester, just like I had, and this was our only connection. He was studying business, I was studying education. He was going into a Masters program, I was going right into public school teaching. He was laidback and cool when it came to me, and I was running hot and at attention when it came to him.

I'm not sure that dating me had really been his idea, honestly. It's far more likely that after his friends saw me chatting and flirting with him half a semester into classes, they bought him a clue and convinced him that he would be crazy to not ask me out. So, he did. And I, of course, said yes.

We were together six years. Six years. Through graduation, through graduate school, and well into real adulthood, with real jobs, real responsibilities, and real life – Jonathan Parker and Sara Wright. For such a long while, he was so much a part of who I was that I couldn't remember... well, who I even was apart from him.

Which is why it had been so easy to become someone completely different than who I had always wanted to be. My big plan had been to be married with a whole horde of children by my thirtieth birthday, but the closer I got to that day with Jon, the less likely he seemed to be able to make those dreams a reality. Common sense would have called me to stop and take stock of where we were, where we were heading, and if we were even still supposed to be together, but I was too far gone, all those years in, to listen to common sense. As time went on and I grew more dependent on him, loving him as wholly and honestly as I had loved anyone in my entire life, I gave him everything I had to give.

I made some mistakes, we made some mistakes, and when his work transferred him to a job two hundred miles away, I appreciated the distance as it gave me a chance to cool off and calm down. And I hoped and prayed that it would give Jon a chance to see that he really needed me by his side, not as what I had become, but as his wife. As time went on, I wanted a commitment, a legitimate reason to follow him wherever he went, and to make our relationship as serious as it had always been in my heart, as serious as my actions had led me to believe it was. Even as he became distant and I began to partially hate him for hurting me, I still clung to the hope that we'd end up married, and I wouldn't have to regret so much time and so much love lost on him.

Then, before I left for Costa Rica, it all fell apart. Katie entered the picture, Jon broke up with me, and last I heard, they were planning on getting married.

Which is why I was perplexed as my parents excused themselves from the chat I had been looking forward to having with them, making room and privacy for Jon to talk with me, as he took special care to adjust their laptop screen with his left hand, showing me in the process that he wore no wedding ring.

We stared at one another for a moment, neither of us saying any of the million things that likely needed to be said.

"Why," I began after more than a few seconds, "are you at my parents' house?"

He smiled. "Well, it's a long story."

"I've got time," I managed.

"I relocated to Dallas a few weeks ago. Tried calling you, but... well, your phone was disconnected." He shook his head. "Didn't really think too much more about it until tonight, when I was driving by your parents' house, stopped in to say hi, and... well, here I am."

Jon had always been a charmer with my parents. They loved him so much and had so mourned his departure from my life last year. Maybe even more than I had, honestly. Which would explain why they had left him alone now, to talk with me.

"They told me that you were in Costa Rica last year," he laughed. "Which was shocking, of course. And then, they told me that you had just moved to Africa, which was even MORE shocking."

"It's been a shock to us all," I murmured, thinking on the past two days. "Believe me."

"But the good news," he said, smiling at me again, "was that I just happened to show up on the same night they were going to be talking to you." He watched me for a moment.

"And here I am," I concluded.

He smiled. "You look amazing, Sara. Really. It's like no time has passed at all, and—"

"How's Katie?," I blurted out before I could stop myself.

He raised his eyebrows. "Ahh, yeah. Katie. Well, she's not here."

"Clearly," I studied him for a moment. "I heard you were getting married."

He crossed his arms on the desk, taking a deep breath. "Yeah... that was the plan. For a while, at least. But I never did."

My mind raced through all the possibilities behind the breakup. More infidelity, boredom, career changes, trust issues –

"I was still in love with you."

Or that.

I must have worn a dubious expression because he clarified with, "Sara, I'm still in love with you."

"What?" My mind clicked through how this could be, when towards the end of our relationship, he had no interest in even seeing me, much less being faithful to me, and how –

"I made some mistakes," he said, lowering his voice. "Some huge mistakes. If I could go back and do it all over again, I would get down on my knees back in that stupid health class and beg you to marry me without any reservations or hesitation *at all*."

"Well," I managed, leaning back in my chair, taking a huge breath. "That would have changed a lot of things, wouldn't it?"

"Hey," he said. "I was wrong. For... for not doing the right thing. Back when you needed me to. And I've gotten my life straightened back out. And I want... to see where this could go."

I watched his face, my eyes drifting over all of the features that I had spent so many years loving, my heart betraying me even as the memories flooded my mind.

"I think about you all the time, Sara," he said softly. "Do you remember all those nights studying at that crappy diner?"

"Note cards," I said, nodding. "Ten thousand note cards I filled out, all on something I didn't understand, to help you study when I should have been working on my own lesson plans."

He smiled at me. "But I helped you, too. All those weekends helping you to decorate your classroom, painting those posters, cutting things out, sitting in those ridiculously tiny chairs –"

"Not so tiny if you're five years old, you know."

He leaned closer to the screen. "And the really good times, too. Kissing you for the first time at the end of your sorority formal, all those July 4th picnics with your family, the night we went to look at all the Christmas lights and ended up driving for four straight hours, until my car ran out of gas and –"

"We had to call Melissa to come and pick us up," I sighed.

"And that weekend," he said, a new expression on his face now, "when your parents were out of town, and you met me out back in the hot tub…"

I looked back down at my hands, my pulse racing at the memory, the shame of the next morning, swearing it would never happen again, then only a week later, the greater shame at his apartment when it did. And again and again, until –

My eyes found his, my resolve strong in this if in nothing else. "I shouldn't have done that. We shouldn't have done it. And not because we fell apart. But because it was wrong. And it made it impossible for me to see you without expecting something I shouldn't have."

His face softened. "You're right. You're absolutely right. But you were right to expect more. And I should have done more. And I want to make it right now. If you'll let me."

"Jon," I said, not even sure how I felt at this point, with all of this new information overwhelming me, "I'm half a world away. Literally."

"I know," he said. "And I understand. But can I... can I keep in touch? At least just keep in touch, and see what happens?"

Six years. I had already given him so much. What was more time here, just seeing what might happen –

"Okay."

"Really?," he asked, smiling.

"Yeah. We can... see what happens."

By the time the call was done, the sun had finally risen in Namibia.

As my mind raced over all that Jon had said, I began setting up my new home, biding my time until I assumed most of the stores in town would finally be open. Still wearing my clothes from the day before, thanks to my stolen luggage, I made my way down to my garage and the truck I didn't trust myself to be able to drive, with plans to replace my wardrobe. Or as much as I could afford to replace.

Before I could get in the truck, my phone rang.

Daniel Boyd.

I took a deep breath, expecting nothing but more animosity from him, before I took the call.

"Hello?"

"Hey. It's Daniel."

"Yes?," I said impatiently.

"Just calling to make sure you're still there this morning," he said. I could almost hear the smile in his voice. "Got back to your flat with the truck, I'm assuming."

"That I did," I said confidently, suddenly certain that I'd be able to drive just fine, if only to spite him. "And now, I'm going shopping."

"Well, look at you. Acting like a proper Swakop tourist already."

Before I could tell him just exactly what I thought about that, he went on.

"Just wanted to tell you... well, that I'm sorry for being so rude yesterday."

"And are you going to call me tomorrow to apologize for *this* phone call?"

A pause. "Am I being rude, Miss Wright?" Oh, he was totally smiling on the other end of the line.

"Yes, indeed, you *are*, Mr.... well, excuse me, *Reverend* Boyd."

"Don't call me Reverend."

"Would you prefer Pastor? Rabbi? Prophet? Vicar? Father? Holy High Exalted Priest —"

He laughed out loud. "Wow, someone is *not* a morning person."

"Why are you even calling me?," I finally spat out, beyond exasperated already.

He sighed. "Just to apologize. Honestly. I should have been... nicer. But, Sara, it's just not in me to be nice most of the time. Why do you think the mission board stuck me out here all by myself?"

"Perhaps they hoped you would be eaten by some African wildlife, huh?"

"Shaaaaame, man," he said, laughing again. "Are you still saying that this morning? Just like your Afrikaner buddies, huh? Shame, man, shame, man..." A pause. "How was dinner?"

"Good, actually," I said leaning against the wall of the garage. "Riaan and Ana Marie seemed a bit shocked to hear about my plans for ministry."

"I can imagine," he said. "Crazy idea, you know. Still a go, though? You're going forward with plans?"

"Just as soon as I can go buy some clothes to wear today," I affirmed, nodding my head at this.

A pause. "Are you naked right now?"

"No," I gasped, blushing at this. "Most of my clothes were stolen, of course, but I still have —"

"Oh!," he said, realization in his voice. "That's right – the stolen luggage. One change of clothes. I remember now." Then, sarcastically, "Wow, there were just *so many* fiascos that happened over the past two days that I'm having trouble remembering them all."

Silence.

"Well?"

"Are you done?," I asked.

"Yeah," he sighed. "I'm done. I'm sorry." Another pause. "So what's the plan for ministry? Honestly, I'd like to hear about it."

"Well, I figure I'll go and meet with some of the local church pastors, figure out if there's any interest towards this kind of project, you know?"

"Sounds good," he said softly. "The local pastors part. The center, of course, sounds bloody awful, but you're going to go ahead with it anyway, despite what I think. All thanks to the mission board."

And there he was yet again – the Daniel from yesterday. Just when I started to feel sorry for wishing him eaten alive by a whole pride of lions

–

"Oh, and while you're at it today," he said, "make sure and adjust the spring on your garage door."

"What?"

"You have to adjust it to the right tension," he explained. "Your flat is brand new, so they've probably never done that before. Until you adjust it, the door can just slam closed, right on your truck."

"Well, I don't think that's going to –" I said, just as the door slammed right down, as if on cue, leaving me in the dark and trapping me inside. "Happen," I finished lamely. Just great.

"Should've done it myself yesterday," Daniel continued on, oblivious to how I was now beginning to panic in the pitch dark. "But with that impromptu driving lesson, I was pressed for time. And as you so painstakingly told me yesterday when you were struggling to learn how to drive, you're man enough to handle anything that comes your way, right? Garage doors and all."

"Uh-huh," I said, feeling my way over to the door, noting with no small amount of dismay that I was now *locked* in my dark garage. Oh, for the love of –

"Anyway," Daniel sighed, "that's all I was calling to tell you."

"Well, I appreciate it," I said, now jumping up and down and shaking the lock myself, fruitlessly. "I really, really appreciate it!," I managed through clenched teeth as I fought the urge to burst into tears.

"Well, you sound like you do," Daniel said. "You call me if you need anything, okay?"

I needed *him*, right then, to come and get me out of here. But figuring that this would cause a relapse back to the frustrated, agitated Daniel Boyd, who surely couldn't help me out today anyway since he was all the way in Windhoek, I simply said, "Okie-dokie."

"Cheers," he offered, then hung up.

And I put my phone down and began screaming.

I finally broke down and called Ana Marie an hour later, after I had exhausted all other efforts and means of freeing myself from the garage, just as I was beginning to doubt that I would ever see the Namibian sun again.

"Shame, man!," she shrieked when she heard my dilemma. "I shall call Riaan and have him pick me up so we can come rescue you!"

They arrived ten minutes later, and Riaan was able to pick the lock from the outside, much to my relief and Ana Marie's boisterous applause.

"This is why I married him," she said, kissing him, then embracing me. "Because things like this? Happen to me *all* the time, Sara."

Riaan grinned at the truth of this. "Sara," he said, "may I fix the spring so that this doesn't happen again?"

"By all means, yes," I said. "Baie dankie, friend."

"Pleasure," he smiled and set to work, as Ana Marie looked over my clothing critically.

"Have you been in there all night?," she asked.

"No, why... oh!," I exclaimed, looking down at my clothes. "Still in the same clothes. Yes, I know." I sighed. "My bags were stolen. I have... well, this. And the clothes I was wearing when I left the US."

"Oh, no!," Ana Marie shouted. "That's a *travesty*."

I was surprised to hear this word come out of her mouth. As if reading my mind, Riaan shouted out, "Ana Marie's favorite English word. Travesty."

"It just sounds like its meaning, ne?," she asked, smiling at me. Before I could respond, she started speaking again, with great animation. "I will bring you some clothes! We are about the same size, ne?"

"Well, yes," I said, "but I had plans today to go shopping."

"Ooooh," she smiled. "May I go with? I love shopping."

I could feel my mood lifting already. "You bet. Wanna drive my truck for me?"


The Bothas were good friends. Very good friends. As I settled into life, into a routine, into a regular day-to-day existence, there in Swakopmund, Ana Marie and Riaan were right with me.

Ana Marie even volunteered to go along with me to visit churches in the area. "Just to translate, in case you need it," she smiled as she offered.

There was no translation needed at the first church we visited. They were an English-speaking congregation in a church right by the sea, and after only ten minutes at their friendly, warm, and welcoming service, I knew it would become my home church. I went forward at the end of the hour to join, leaving Ana Marie by herself for a moment. When I joined her again, after speaking with the pastor, I was surprised to find her surrounded by several senior adult ladies, all of them chattering away in animated Afrikaans. Each of them embraced Ana Marie enthusiastically, then me, as introductions were made and farewells were exchanged.

"What was that about?," I asked her, grinning.

"I have no idea," she said, laughing. "Who knew born again people were so friendly?"

I shrugged as we made our way outside together.

"Come have lunch with Riaan and me, Sara," Ana Marie said as we climbed into my truck. "Riaan has made a lovely braai this morning, I imagine."

"A braai?," I asked as I started the truck effortlessly.

"I don't know the English word for it," she said, her eyes dancing, "but it's wonderful. You will enjoy it *and* the company, of course."

"No doubt, friend."

We were an hour into the braai (which was a barbecue, in English terms), when Ana Marie dropped the bombshell on her husband.

"Riaan, lovey, we should be going to church with Sara," she said in her spirited, animated way.

A look of horror crossed Riaan's face. "What?"

"I want to go to church," she said simply, with a wave of her hand, as though this was some fantastical, whimsical decision that she had reached while in a daze.

Riaan looked to me. I shrugged.

"I wasn't aware that she felt like that," I managed. "It's the first I've heard. But you two could always go to church with me. Or, you know, somewhere else if you want to."

"No, we want to go with *you*," Ana Marie said. "The people there were just so kind, Riaan. We should go there, too."

"Ana Marie —"

"Riaan," she said sweetly, glancing over at me.

"Sara," he said, "My hard feelings are not about... Jesus. But the church is... well, not the kind of place I want to be. They've done some awful things, you see?"

And while I didn't know what Riaan's personal bias was against the church, I could guess some of the reasons, because they were common enough, no matter where in the world you were.

"People aren't perfect," I said, succinctly.

"Ja," Riaan agreed. "And the church people are proof of that."

"Riaan, *we* are proof of that," Ana Marie chided.

He looked at her. "Ana Marie, jy moet nie –"

"*Eish!*," she exclaimed, "I should, and I will. We are not perfect, lovey. And the people in the church do not have to be *perfect*. But the ladies today were so kind and sweet, just like our good friend, Sara." She leaned forward and lowered her voice meaningfully, "Who, Riaan, is *in the church*."

"Shame, Sara," Riaan said, "I did not mean to say that *you* are a... um, someone who says one very good thing and does something very bad..."

"A hypocrite?," I supplied helpfully.

"Ja!," he nodded.

"Oh, but I am, Riaan," I sighed.

Both Bothas looked at me curiously.

"Could you say that again, Sara?," Ana Marie asked.

"I'm a hypocrite," I said. "I say one thing and do another, all the time. And I'm just as bad as all the people who've likely driven you from the church, Riaan."

"I don't think that's possible," he began.

"It is. But that's why I need Jesus. And all those people? Need Jesus. You need Him, too, Riaan. And it's a real shame that you're letting all the hypocrites out there keep you from Him."

It was about the most ineloquent testimony I'd ever given, but Riaan was speechless. He and Ana Marie exchanged a glance, and I took a deep breath, sensing that some things were better left to time.

"Shame, man," I said, smiling. "Let me help you clear out these dishes, huh?"

# 3 CHAPTER THREE

The center? Wasn't coming together like I had hoped.

No one was willing to help. Absolutely no one.

I had been by literally every church in Swakopmund, looking for a believer somewhere, anywhere, who had a heart for what was happening in our own backyard. While many were moved by the conditions there, none were moved enough towards compassion to do anything more than a soup kitchen once a quarter.

But it would come… right? Surely. I acted on faith although there was clearly no evidence of any of it being sight at this point, locating the warehouse that would serve as a workspace and storage area that would become the center, setting about getting supplies shipped and purchased, and making arrangements with those back in the US who were partnering with me in this project.

The rest of my time I spent visiting with the Bothas, getting my bearings about me in this new place, getting the center ready, and praying. Praying everywhere, all the time, in any and every situation. Even if I couldn't hit the ground running, like I had in Costa Rica, I could pray. And I could wait for the opportunities that would come.

It would happen, this project, all these opportunities to share the Gospel...

Wouldn't it?

I was in the midst of one of those long evenings of prayer when Ana Marie showed up at my front door, hysterical.

"What's wrong?," I asked, concerned, after I had brought her in, sat her down, and handed her a box of tissues.

"*Riaan!*," she moaned. "He's what is *wrong*! He's a *monster*!"

I couldn't imagine mild, even-mannered Riaan as any kind of monster, but I listened as she continued bemoaning his shortcomings.

"He does not understand what it is *like*, Sara. Moving away from home, being here in this.... place, without family around."

Ana Marie had grown up in South Africa and had moved to Namibia to marry Riaan, who had his business here. She had a very charmed life – living as a homemaker who spent her days shopping and spending the money her husband worked hard to earn –

"He said I needed to stop *shopping* so much!"

Ahh.

"Are you shopping because... you miss home?," I asked, trying to understand how the two were connected.

"Shame, man, no," she said, blowing her nose. "It's just what else am I going to do with my time, you know? But he does not understand, you see, because he has this ongelooflike life, flying the tourists around and all."

I had no idea what that meant, but context clues were enough to paint a picture for me. "Did you tell him this?"

"Ja," she nodded, "and he told me it did not matter. And that I needed to get a hobby instead of spending all of the money at the shops."

"Shame."

"Ja!," she exclaimed. "It is like I do not even *know* this man I married! It has only been three months, and he is like a stranger, you know? He does not want me to spend money, he does not understand how I am so lonely, and…. Sara," she said, lowering her voice, "he dreams in *English*." She burst into tears all over again. "Talks in his sleep in *English*, thanks to that aaklig mother of his!"

"Why is it his mother's fault?," I asked.

"Because she is *English*!," Ana Marie screeched. "I could not even marry a proper Afrikaner, Sara!"

I let her cry for a moment. Then, praying while I contemplated the words I was about to say, I told her, "I think… you are concerned about many things, Ana Marie."

"Ja," she said. "Don't ever get married, Sara, because men are no good."

"I don't think that's true," I told her. "Because you? Are married to a very good man."

She rolled her eyes at this. "If you think so, then perhaps *you* should try living with him."

"Shame," I smiled, "I think he's just having a hard time understanding you… you know? Relationships are hard, and you two are so very different already. And now, you're in a new place, in a stressful new phase of life, and… well, I can see why it would be hard for you both."

"He will not *try* to understand where I am coming from, Sara," Ana Marie huffed. "He will never completely understand how I feel!"

I thought about this for a moment. "You're right," I said.

"Pardon?," she asked, wiping her nose.

"Well, you're right. He probably won't ever completely understand you," I sighed. "I think you're expecting Riaan to do what only God can do. Riaan can't understand you the way you always need to be understood, and he certainly can't be whoever you need him to be."

"And you think God can? Or that He would want to?," she said doubtfully. "Sara, I'm not even sure how that all works anyway."

I shrugged. "I'm not sure either, but I know that you need to find your fulfillment in Christ, not in Riaan."

Ana Marie watched me, shocked for a moment. Then, she asked, quietly, "Why are you here, Sara, coming all this way by yourself, to tell people things like this?," she asked, wonder on her face. "I'm sure you have better things to do."

"I can think of no better place to be, right now, than here with you, talking about these things," I said to her, sincerely meaning it. Then, after another thoughtful moment, "And I think... that if Jesus Himself was here right now, He would want nothing more than to spend an evening, just being with you."

She looked at me with tears in her eyes. "Do you really think that?," she whispered.

I smiled. "Actually, I know that."


The Bothas made up the next morning. And I was privy to just what that looked like later on that afternoon, when we all three met up at the beach, and the two of them were all over one another. Just as I was about to excuse myself to leave them to their groping and gazing, Riaan smiled over at me.

"Sara, how are your plans for the DRC going?"

I put down the bottle of sunscreen I had been using. "Not so good, actually," I breathed out. "I have the supplies, the building, and plans, but…. no people to help."

"Shame," Ana Marie said, climbing out of Riaan's lap to sit next to me on my beach towel. "There are *plenty* of people to help there. More than plenty."

"Yes," I sighed. "But I can't speak with any of them. I mean, literally. I don't speak the language."

"Lovey," Riaan said, looking to Ana Marie, "you should use some of your free time to go and help Sara. Be her translator."

I hadn't considered Ana Marie as an option before. I looked to her, wondering what her reaction would be, and my heart leapt to see her smile.

"Ja!," she yelled. "Hanging out with Sara, chatting all day… could be better than shopping, ne, Riaan?"

"Better for my wallet, most definitely," he laughed, kissing her.


To: Sara Wright (sarawright@gonowmissions.org)

From: Daniel Boyd (danielboyd@gonowmissions.org)

Subject: Bibles

Sara,

I got your request for ONE Afrikaans Bible. At the risk of seeming overly optimistic about whatever it is you're doing out there in your holiday town, I'm actually going to ship an entire case of Afrikaans Bibles to you.

Not that I think you're going to need that many.

Okay, so maybe I hope you will.

Let me know what's going on when you get the chance, okay? Praying for you.

Daniel

Ana Marie was amazing.

The center became her hobby. It was her respite from homesickness and her prevention against shopping. She went beyond simple translation, though. She was a one-woman show in the DRC, charming and befriending the women, setting them up on a schedule, arranging transport with them, and then, helping once we got the center going. She did everything except share the Gospel with them, which I saw as an opportunity to share the Gospel with *her*.

"What is this?," she asked when I handed her the large book, just as our first group of ladies was settling in to make some simple bracelets.

"You tell me," I said. "I can't read it."

She smiled, looking at the cover, then flipping the book open to browse some of the pages. "You have found a Bible for me?," she asked, confusion on her face.

"Yes," I said. "So that you might share some stories with the ladies. I can't read them myself, unfortunately, but I thought they might enjoy hearing you read them. You have such a lovely voice."

"Sara," she sighed, "that is very sweet. Come now, show me which story I shall read today."

I led her to John 3:16, easy enough to find even in Afrikaans.

"This," I said, pointing to the verse. "It's something that Jesus said. Perhaps you've heard it?"

She read it out loud to me. "God het die wereld so liefgehad dat Hy sy enigste Seun gegee het, sodat die wat in Hom glo, nie verlore sal gaan nie maar die ewige lewe sal he." Then, gasping out loud, "Shame, man! Was Jesus Afrikaans?!"

I smiled. "No, but... well, He understands you, Ana Marie. And needs no translation."

She flipped through the Bible, marveling over the words written there. "My language... I shall treasure these words, Sara. Truly, I will."


In no time at all, from the small beginnings of visits to the DRC, to the arrangements discussed, to the simple help of a friend who came alongside me, and to all the difference she made... the center was up and running to full capacity. Better than I had imagined or envisioned, honestly.

And the work was life changing. As I had prayed it would be.

There was Ana Marie, of course, who helped out more and more every week, seeming to find more joy in the task at hand and the visitation that went along with it than I would certainly have predicted she would. She was a breath of sunshine in the warehouse we were renting, greeting and talking with the ladies in her animated, excited way, working alongside them with such vivacity and enthusiasm that she quickly became someone they confided in and trusted, even more than they probably trusted me. They loved her so completely for many reasons...

... and one of the most compelling reasons was Riaan.

I had known he was kind, gentle, and sweet from the moment I met him, but as Ana Marie became more involved with the center's work and had him visit with her from time to time, when he was in between flights with work, I saw how deep his kindness was. He took great interest in each of the women, in their children, in their lives, and in doing all that he could practically to help with all they struggled with in the DRC. It wasn't unusual to find him bringing medicine, sending the ladies back with special treats for their children, or speaking affirmations over them. Many of these ladies had never been shown any kindness from any man, especially not any white man, and Riaan, with his surprisingly gentle and genuine spirit, seemed to profoundly move them.

And Riaan, it seemed, was profoundly moved himself.

"Sara," he said to me one afternoon, "I'm thinking more and more that it's a good thing that you came to Namibia."

I smiled. "The work is meaningful, isn't it?"

"Ja, it is," he sighed. "And that's just at the humanitarian level. Though I know you have deeper reasons for doing what you do."

"That I do," I murmured.

"I've been... reading," he said. "Reading the Bible you gave Ana Marie. And perhaps... there is more to your deeper reason. I'm not sure myself, but I'm trying to sort it all out."

I took a deep breath at the truth of this.

"I think that's the best any of us can do," I affirmed quietly. "Trying to sort out this mystery of... well, grace."

He nodded very simply at this and went back to helping us with our work, a faint smile on his face.


I had my hands full when he called. Literally.

We'd been hard at work all morning, and I'd been right there in the midst of it all, speaking to the women, listening as Ana Marie translated, and enjoying one of many wonderful conversations I'd been able to have with them during those weeks. I had wire, strings, beads, clasps, and tools spread out in front of me and over half of it all in my outstretched hands.

"Excuse me," I said softly, laying the work down gently, and answering my phone. "Hello?"

"Hey. It's Daniel."

I heard from him periodically, mainly to discuss administrative details that he was working through in Windhoek for the work in Swakopmund... or rather, listening to him bark out information about the administrative details. Short, to the point conversations and even shorter, more to the point emails – this was the extent of my communication with the rest of the "team." I braced myself for more of the same.

"Yes," I sighed. "What do you need?"

"How are you?"

I was a bit taken aback by this. "Well... um, fine. I guess." A pause. "How are you?"

"Me?"

"Yeah."

Another pause. "I'm awesome, actually."

"Oh?," I said, wondering at this, since he never seemed to be anything but grumpy. "That's surprising."

"What? You don't think I'm awesome?," he laughed. I could hear his smile... hinting that perhaps he was a nice guy after all. Maybe. Or not.

Most likely not.

"Well, you could be," I said, smiling myself. "But I haven't seen evidence of it. Only of you being supremely annoyed."

"Yeah. Probably." A pause. "But you'll think I'm awesome after I tell you the good news."

"And the good news would be?"

"I need your bank account number."

Well, that was odd. "Why do you need my bank account number?"

"Because," he said, another smile in his voice, "I filed an insurance claim on your stolen luggage, and they paid up. They need your bank account number to wire you the money."

"You did... what?"

He sighed. "Stolen luggage. Claim filed. Money granted. What's hard to understand about this?"

"I didn't even know that... well, that we were insured for something like that."

"Oh, *we* are. And *we* personally have been for the past decade. And this is the first time I've ever had reason to file a claim at all." A pause. "They owe me. Trust me."

"Well," I said carefully, "I don't really need the money to replace everything now. I've already done that. I'm fine."

A long pause. "You mean to tell me that I'm offering you money to go shopping and you have no *need* for it?"

It did sound bizarre, but.... "Yeah. I'm low maintenance. It was a real chore to have to shop earlier."

Ana Marie shot me a troubled look at this, obviously eavesdropping. My speaking ill of shopping was all but blasphemous to her.

"Sara," Daniel said, just a hint of frustration in his voice, "do you know how hard I had to work to get this money? How much paperwork I had to fill out?"

"I appreciate your efforts, honestly, but I don't need the money. I mean, I was able to replace all that I needed on –"

"You deserve the money. As payment for the trauma you went through in losing your luggage," he insisted.

"Trauma?," I began. "Well, that's a bit much, and –"

"Sara, I need you to *take the money.*"

A pause. "Why?"

He blew out a very frustrated breath. "Here, I am, trying to be a nice guy, and you're fighting me every step of the way, and –"

"Daniel." This much was true. He was *trying.* And I wasn't being appreciative of his efforts, which I knew must have been quite costly to him. Not financially but in goodwill points, which he didn't have in large supply anyway, and –

"What?," he spat out. Ahh, there was the Daniel I remembered.

"I appreciate it. Thank you. Let me get my bank information for you."

After I had given him all the details, he took another breath. "You don't have to go buy clothes with it, you know."

"I don't?"

"No," he said, very simply. "I can appreciate someone being low maintenance."

"Thank you."

"Go throw yourself a big party on the money. Eat steak every night for a month."

"That's not really low maintenance," I said, smiling again.

My smile grew when I heard him laugh. "No, probably not. Then, do something noble, Sara. Something great. Okay? Your money, your call."

And as I looked over the ladies gathered there and Ana Marie shot me a questioning, amused look, I began forming a plan.

"Thanks, Daniel. I'll let you know how it turns out."

"This is a crazy idea," Riaan said to me as we drove towards the DRC.

We were just one of many in the caravan of cars heading over there on that particular day. I had taken the money that had shown up in my account – the amount of which was much larger than I had anticipated, thanks to Daniel's persistence – and arranged a soup kitchen day with the members of my church. Riaan and Ana Marie, given how involved they already were with the ladies at the DRC, had opted to come along and help, and the center ladies had arranged everything on their end. It would be quite the soup kitchen...

... because it was more than soup. Fresh fruit, bread, bottled water, medicine, hygiene products – all of them in great supply, loaded up into bakkies, grouped together to hand out to families as they came. It would be a blessing, as would be the message our church members were prepared to individually share with families who came, about the love of God, the mercy of Christ, and the grace that was theirs for the taking.

"It probably is crazy," I agreed with him. "Ana Marie, are you ready to share the Gospel?"

"Ja," she trilled enthusiastically. "Been practicing, you know."

I had taken her and Riaan through the simple presentation, left them to translate it, and had prepared them to share, if all of our volunteers weren't enough. They were excited to do so, even if they themselves still hadn't professed faith.

As we pulled up into the DRC and saw our ladies already organizing people for the pickup of the supplies, we all three took a deep breath as I said a quick prayer out loud.

"Let's go!," Ana Marie exclaimed, before jumping out of the car and rushing to the crowds.

It was like Christmas. Christmas in the middle of the desert.

The gifts were readily accepted with laughter and cheering, even with singing and dancing, and the church volunteers were better than I had ever hoped, being the hands and feet of Christ in tangible, real ways.

I watched it all from behind the lens of my camera, snapping picture after picture of children being fed, women being blessed, men hearing the Gospel, and the body of Christ functioning as it had been commissioned to do.

Ana Marie and Riaan were amazing, as I had known they would be. Embracing our ladies and their families, handing out supplies, and sharing what I had taught them. At one point, Ana Marie scurried off with her Bible, leaving Riaan looking perplexed and concerned with his inability to recall the Scriptures I had highlighted for them.

I was prepared for even this.

"Riaan!," I shouted, reaching into my backpack, my hand finding one of the many Bibles Daniel had shipped to me, with little expectation that they would ever be used. "Take this one!"

And I tossed it to him. He caught it in one hand, smiling at me. "Now, I suppose I shall have to read it as much as Ana Marie does, ne?"

"Ja, friend," I smiled.

And he smiled back as I took another picture.

It was a mountaintop experience. We had enough. The money had been enough. God had stretched it into enough so that no one was left unsatisfied in the DRC, at least for that day. The church went home, revitalized and encouraged, excited about more opportunities to share and minister. The Bothas went home, thrilled to have done something so incredible, talking so animatedly with one another that they didn't even think to speak in English to me.

And I went home. Alone.

Here's the thing about mountaintop experiences – you have to come down off the mountain eventually. And I was finding that more often than not, my mountains were surrounded by valleys, lower and deeper and darker than any I had known before. Life changing ministry in Namibia, things I had never imagined God capable of in my comfortable life in the States... followed by bleak, dismal loneliness as I was acutely aware of being by myself.

Life was lonely. I was lonely. And just as I looked at my phone and began to wonder at who I could call, if there was anyone in all the world who would even care to hear about what I had just experienced, it rang in my hands.

Jon.

I answered apprehensively.

I had spoken to him since the night of the chat. I had spoken to him more times than I had been able to keep count. And in those conversations, there was a quiet desperation in me, to be heard and understood... and yet, at the same time, there was an unsettling lack of peace. Jon was who he had been, was everything I had spent so many years loving... but something was different.

Perhaps it was *me*.

This wasn't the time to figure it out, though. This was a God-given moment to share what mattered most to me, to tell him what had happened, to let Jon see what was in my heart at this very moment –

"Sara..."

"Hey, Jon," I breathed. "How are you?"

"Tired," he said, laughing. "It's the middle of the night."

I looked at my watch. "Shame, man, that it is. What are you doing awake?"

"I set my alarm," he said. "Set it so that I could call you at a decent hour for *you*."

I smiled at this. "Well, that's thoughtful. I thought maybe you were calling because of the soup kitchen."

A pause, longer than the international delay called for. "Soup kitchen?"

"Yeah," I said, a little dismayed that he could have forgotten about this when it was all I had been able to think about. "Remember? The insurance money? I spent it to take food and medicine and –"

"Did you seriously end up doing that?," Jon asked, incredulously.

It had been uncalled for generosity. To the point of being foolish, actually, and I knew it. But it was a privilege. And I smiled, knowing that this is exactly what Jon would see and that his exclamation would be for all the good that had been done and not the cost –

"I wish you had kept the money and used it for a plane ticket to come home for a visit," he breathed out.

I thought about what a trip back home would mean for me. About how welcome it would be, to be surrounded by the familiar, by friends, by family, by all that I had been. To come back to Namibia with an engagement ring on my finger, likely, the promise of all that I had spent so many years dreaming and hoping for a certain, imminent reality.

And then, I thought about the tiny children in the DRC who had begun eating the food the very second we placed it in their hands, some of the smallest of the bunch clinging to me as I kissed their heads and wiped away my tears, all while whispering prayers over them.

Spending all the money had been no sacrifice, not in light of this.

But Jon didn't know it. He sighed again. "I just miss you, Sara. That's all. I wish you'd think more about yourself and what you want than making all of those people over there happy, you know?"

And there it was. The unsettling lack of peace. About him. About us.

Before I could address it or could begin to share how amazing it had been to see that money bless so many, materially and spiritually, he continued on.

"So, I've got this new project going on at work that I wanted to tell you about…"

And I scarcely spoke another word for the rest of the conversation.


To: Sara Wright (sarawright@gonowmissions.org)

From: Daniel Boyd (danielboyd@gonowmissions.org)

Subject: Re: DRC Project

Sara,

I got the pictures you sent. Along with the explanation of how you managed to finance such a wild, ill-conceived, over-the-top party in the DRC with your blatant misuse of that insurance money. Dangerous, naive, and completely irresponsible, going there like that with such lavish intentions.

My thoughts on what you did? In one word?

AWESOME.

I'm keeping the picture of you, surrounded by all those smiling children, right here on my desk next to the stack of ever-present expense reports staring me in the face. It'll be a good reminder of what real ministry looks like here in Namibia.

Thanks.

Daniel


Ana Marie was, by her own admission, a little stressed out.

"Riaan has some questions," she told me one afternoon over tea time. "Well, and so do I. But he's been reading the Bible you gave him. *A lot.* And he just… well, we've just never heard any of the things in there. And now, we're reading, and Riaan is… well, he's talking about how God is *speaking* to him, and…" She threw her hands into the air. "I'm just really confused about it all, Sara!"

And though I had prayed for this… I was a bit confused as well. I wasn't sure how prepared I was to lead the Bothas through the conversations that were to be had, the questions that were coming up, and the realizations they were making on their own, thanks to the counsel of

Scripture and my ineloquent explanations, interpretations, and direction.

I had no answers for Riaan when it came to some of the bigger questions that were plaguing him. These questions seemed to remain as the final roadblocks between him and faith, between his wife and faith, and as I stressed over how to help them surpass these monumental mysteries of faith, I went to a default I hadn't known I was relying on. With Ana Marie and Riaan there at my flat, waiting anxiously, I called him.

He picked up on the third ring, exasperation in his voice.

"Yes?"

A breath. "Daniel?"

"Ahh, Miss Wright." Great. He was in a mood. A Daniel mood.

"It's Sara. And I have a huge favor to ask. Are you busy right now?"

"Yeah," he spat out. "Up to my elbows in expense reports. Why the board needs these things done all the time, I'll never know, but I guess we just have to do it, like the mindless drones that we are, huh, Miss Wright? I mean, Sara. Well, actually, *you* don't have to do any of them, what with your fabulous life seaside as the —"

"Daniel?"

A breath from him this time. "I'm sorry. But, yes, I'm busy. If you hadn't already gathered."

I glanced over at the Bothas, who looked to me eagerly. I was thankful that they couldn't hear the conversation.

"Shame, man, I understand. I'm sorry I called," I said. "Perhaps another time?"

"Well, you might as well tell me *why* you called."

"I... I have some friends who... who have some questions. About God. And I'm feeling a little ill-equipped to answer..."

Silence. "You want me to answer their questions?"

"Well... yeah. If you have time."

"Sure, sure," he said, his voice softening, causing me to look at the phone with no small amount of wonder and... well, alarm, frankly. "This?," he continued on, "is why I'm here. To explain these things, not fill out expense reports. I'm glad you called, Sara. Honestly."

This made me smile. "Good. Well... they're here right now, if you want to..."

"Put them on the line," he said.

"Actually, I'm going to put you on speakerphone," I said, pushing a button. "Daniel, are you still there?"

"Yeah. Can you hear me?"

I told him I could, then made introductions around the room. Then, just as we were all falling into silence, I looked to Riaan.

"Ja," he said, a little anxiously. "Sara has been telling us a lot. And answering many questions. And I have been reading a lot as well, and... well, I guess the question that remains unanswered for me is... why, if God is so good, did He even allow sin to begin with? Why did He make it so that we would be separated from Him? And why, if He loves us as much as Sara says He does, did He have to turn His back on us, then die to save us? Couldn't He just make it right without all of that?"

I blew out a breath. That was more than one question, obviously. Just as I was wondering if Daniel could even begin to formulate a response, he began speaking... in perfect Afrikaans.

And both Bothas listened intently. As Daniel continued on, passionately and energetically, in an accent that sounded just exactly like theirs, in words that their hearts certainly understood better than my English ones, realization and understanding washed over their faces. They asked more questions, which Daniel answered easily. He spent at least ten minutes explaining these things to them, pausing as Riaan would look things up in his Bible, as Ana Marie read them aloud, and then as they both listened to his thoughts. And his voice softened, and though I couldn't understand the words, I had no problem translating the care and concern, the compassion and kindness in his delivery. Ana Marie wiped some tears away as Riaan nodded, finally, it seemed, satisfied with the answers he'd be given.

"Sara, are you still there?," Daniel asked, switching back to his brisk, efficient English.

"Yeah," I said, emotional myself as I watched the Bothas discuss these things quietly with one another, no longer listening to Daniel and me. I took him off of speakerphone. "I'm here. And you're off speakerphone."

"Thanks for calling me," he said softly. "I think your friends are... well, a little less confused."

If he could have seen them then, smiling at one another and whispering with such excitement, he would have known it was more than just a little clarity, and –

"I just want to warn you," he said, cutting into my thoughts, "that it's a long road for most from these questions to conversions. And your friend, Riaan? From what he told me, he's been burned by the church in the past, so it might *never* work out for him. Those are hard walls to break through."

"Oh, I don't know," I said, watching as Riaan looked down at the Bible in his hands with a new softness in his eyes, noting that already the cover and the binding were looking well worn and well loved.

"You just keep on keeping on," Daniel continued, oblivious to what God was doing. "I've got to get back to those expense reports now."

"Thanks again, Daniel."

"No problem. Seriously."

Riaan and Ana Marie figured it out together. And the two of them showed up at my flat early one morning, before I'd even had a chance to properly wake up, their faces excited as they pounded on my front door.

"I'm coming, I'm coming," I shouted, opening the door to them, then stepping aside as they barreled in.

"Sara!," Ana Marie trilled. "We need to speak with you!"

"Apparently," I said. "And it must be important since it's not even… 6 am." I gave them an incredulous look as they made themselves at home on my couch, sitting side by side, holding hands. I made my way over to the opposite couch, sat down, and looked to them expectantly.

"We believe it, Sara," Riaan said softly. "Every word of Scripture. Every word that He said. We believe it."

"And it changes things," Ana Marie whispered. "It changes everything. And we want to be more than we've been, for His sake, for His glory."

I sat, staring at them dumbfounded, remembering Daniel's words about how long this might take, and –

"Well?," Riaan said. "Did we… not say it right in English?"

"Shame," Ana Marie murmured. "Perhaps we should just say… we are born again? Does that make better sense, Sara?"

I shook myself out of my stupor. "You were making perfect sense, friends," I managed, a smile suddenly beginning to bloom on my face. "Wonderfully perfect sense."

"What can we do?," Riaan asked. "We want to be who God wants us to be here. What do we do? Where can we help?"

"Well," I said, amazed at what God had already done, "how do you feel about continuing on with work in the DRC? Alongside me?"

Daniel was, in a word, perplexed when I shared my news with him over the phone.

"They want to be baptized," I said. "They... I... well, I've never baptized anyone! Do I have to be, you know, licensed or ordained or... well, something? Can *you* come out and help me?" I thought back to all the ladies won to the Lord in Costa Rica, how I had never had a situation like this because Bryan and Christy had always been there with me, along with countless other kind and supportive missionaries, all of whom were ready and able to baptize, disciple, and completely come alongside new believers as they made decisions.

Somehow, this was different. Mainly because Daniel was having a hard time even believing me.

"Are you serious about this? You've only been there... three months! And you're already baptizing someone?"

"I haven't baptized anyone!," I said. "We were just talking and spending time together, and... Daniel, I've never seen anything like this happen before! And I've been in church my whole life, have been walking with Christ since I was a little girl, and this? This is... well, unbelievable."

"Well, it happens," he said. "God is already at work, and some clueless missionary shows up, and —"

"Thank you for that," I muttered.

"Oh, Sara, lighten up. This is good news, you know," he managed with a small laugh. "What you should do now is get them involved in a church. In *your* church. Which one did you decide on joining?"

"The one on Vineta."

"Oh, great pastor there. Take the Bothas with you to church, introduce them to the members, to the pastor. He'll know how to counsel them through this decision, and there will be people who are equipped to come alongside them… probably even people who speak their heart language who can properly explain this to them, better than you and I could."

"Praise God for that," I said.

A pause, then humor in his voice. "I still can't believe I'm having this talk with you. You're supposed to be making jewelry, not disciples."

I smiled. "Maybe this crazy project is God's way of doing more than we imagined."

"Maybe so."

To: Sara Wright (sarawright@gonowmissions.org)

From: Emily Morales (emorales@gracecommunity.com)

Sara,

I was so excited to hear about your friends! Isn't this just such amazing, wonderful confirmation that you're right where you need to be? That God knew exactly what He was doing when He sent you to Namibia?

I so get what you said in your last email about feeling lonely, though. About how even with such great friends, it can still be lonely. Be careful, okay? I'm sure it would be that much easier to reach out to the wrong person or the wrong people, feeling that way. And I want you to protect your heart.

Okay, so I'm sounding like an annoying sister, right? Josh is telling me that I'm right on, though. Oh, excuse me, not about the whole protecting your heart thing but about how I'm annoying like a sister. Really, Josh? Really?

So, since he won't stop reading over my shoulder, I'm closing this email. I'll write back soon. Promise.

Love,

Emily


It was the first time I had seen Daniel since my arrival in Swakopmund. He came to the coast after speaking with my Namibian pastor, who had been so eager and excited about the upcoming baptism. I had been eager and excited about it as well, as had Daniel...

... but no one was more excited than the Bothas. They both practically ran into the ocean, screeching at how cold it was, then holding hands, exhilarated, as our pastor prayed over them, speaking to the decision they had made and the savior whom they now belonged to. Down in the water they both went, then up again with triumphant fists in the air, even as Ana Marie jumped in Riaan's arms, sending him underwater again unintentionally.

I could hardly see beyond the tears that fell from my eyes as I laughed with delight, but I still didn't miss seeing Daniel as he stood on the outskirts of the group, smiling to himself. He caught my eye and shrugged, as if to tell me that He had no idea what God was doing in Swakopmund.

It was only the beginning.

"So, I'm impressed by your driving skills," Daniel managed, a smile sneaking onto his face as I drove him across town to the facility I had rented for the center.

"No thanks to my teacher," I said, biting back a smile myself.

"Mmm," he nodded, watching the coastline. "Get much downtime out here?"

"Not too much," I sighed. "But now that the Bothas are going to be helping out with the work at the center even more, maybe I'll have some free time. Or maybe not. Who knows?" I thought on this for a moment, about how the work was so immense, how there were never many opportunities for rest... only at night, late after everyone else had gone on to their warm homes, and I went back to spend all of my evenings alone, in my cold, empty flat.

"You need to take breaks," Daniel said, simply. "Otherwise, you'll become – this," he said, indicating himself.

"Perhaps you should take a break," I said, glancing over at him.

"I would, but –"

"No time," we said together.

He smiled at me wryly. "I'm planning a trip up to the north. Soon. I'm thinking I might take some time at the end of that. Maybe come down here, too. Just to make sure you're still standing strong, you know?"

"Standing strong?," I asked him doubtfully.

"It's lonely out here," he said, glancing back at the road, crossing his arms over his chest. "That's one of the reasons Mr. Shiftoka would have been the perfect missionary."

"Ahh, Mr. Shiftoka," I muttered. It would be a welcome day when I never had to hear the name of the much-anticipated, long-coveted Mr.

Shiftoka, who left the door wide open for me to come to Namibia and ruin all of Daniel's plans, as he was oft inclined to tell me again and again and again and –

"He has family here," Daniel said simply. "Not like you. All by yourself. Lonely, lonely, lonely…"

I slammed on the brakes, causing the truck to die. Of course.

"Ah, there are the driving skills I remember," Daniel smiled.

"What are you trying to say?," I hissed.

"You can't drive," he said, mock innocence on his face.

"Oh, no, not that. About the lonely, lonely, lonely thing. Are you trying to run me off again?"

"No," he said, genuine surprise on his face. "I just meant to say that… well, it's lonely. I get that."

"I haven't said a WORD about being lonely here," I said. Although I had certainly felt it. Worse than he could probably imagine, honestly. Sometimes the nights were so lonely that I found myself inexplicably calling Jon, even though I knew it was probably unwise and that I would tell him that I cared more than I probably did, and –

"Well, you're doing better than me, then," Daniel managed. "That's one thing that hasn't changed in all these years for me. How lonely it can get."

I was shocked by this rare moment of vulnerability from him. Before I could say anything in return, before I could tell him that – yes – I understood it, too, he blew out an exasperated breath and said, "Are we just going to sit out here forever, or are you planning on starting the truck again?"

After checking over the building and rebuking my "elementary efforts" at security ("you need new locks, bars on the windows, and a security system," he had said), Daniel let me take him back to his truck where we exchanged an awkward goodbye. Had something changed this afternoon? I couldn't quite pinpoint what it was, but my mind drifted back to his comments about being lonely, about the expression on his face as he said it, about –

And my phone began ringing.

Daniel waved to me, appearing almost relieved for a reason to get in his truck and drive back to Windhoek. I sat on the seawall, sighed, and answered the call.

"Hello?"

A pause. A call from home, then. "Hey, Sara."

Jon.

"Hey... I was just thinking about you." Mainly about how I don't know why I'm still talking to you and what my reasons are for telling you things like this, and –

"Really? I've been thinking about you all night."

And so it continued on, this talk of thoughts, of memories, and of loneliness that stretched far beyond my seaside town.

And I wondered why my mind kept going back to Daniel.

# 4 CHAPTER FOUR

"Sara, I need to talk with you."

It was another day of work at the center. Riaan had spent the better part of the morning arranging transportation with the ladies, and Ana Marie had been at the center all day, working on painting beads for another set of necklaces that had been ordered. The demand for product was high, the opportunities for ministry were growing, and the Bothas were stretching their wings in the DRC, sharing, planning, and imagining even bigger days up ahead.

I wondered if this was on Ana Marie's mind as she asked to speak with me, stretching her back as she stood after so many hours of bending over to work.

"You're going to have back problems, friend," I told her.

"Shame, man, that's the least of my problems," she said, smiling. "I just heard that my brother is coming up from Cape Town."

This is the first I had ever heard of her family coming to visit. "Fun! A visit from family."

She frowned.

"Oh... is this not a good thing?"

"No, it is not," she sighed, "because my brother drives me completely crazy. And what's more? He drives Riaan completely crazy."

I laughed at this. "Well, then, perhaps he shouldn't be coming here, huh?"

"That's what I told him, but he is insistent." Then, taking a deep breath, she continued. "See, he's a pilot as well, just like Riaan. He was the reason Riaan and I met to begin with, actually. But it's been years since then, and they've had a falling out since, and... well, it's just not a pleasant situation. And now, Willem – that's my brother, you see – is looking for work after some... well, some unpleasantness at his last job. I don't know the details, Sara, and I don't *want* to know the details. Willem is a... well, he's... well, I don't even know the English word for what he is." She lowered her voice. "He's not like Riaan." She gave me a meaningful look.

I, of course, had no idea what any of this meant until Willem Kotze showed up the very next day. I had promised that, in an effort to help diffuse the tension between the two men in Ana Marie's life, I would join them for dinner that first night he arrived in town. I walked over to the Botha house as the sun went down, reasoning that Riaan could drive me back, giving himself a break from his brother-in-law if need be. I knocked on the door and smiled when I saw Ana Marie's relieved face.

"Ahh, praise God," she managed. "Willem is already at it." She pulled me in, linked her arm with mine, and continued whispering to me. "At least with you here, he'll be distracted –"

"What –"

"And if not distracted enough, being forced to speak English will at least delay all the stupid, idiotic things that he's likely to say because he'll have to *think* through it before just blurting it out, and –"

She stopped short when we rounded the corner. Riaan was sitting at the table with a blank, glassy eyed look on his face. He glanced over to me with no small measure of relief, which, of course, caused me to direct my own gaze to the problem at hand –

Who had already stood to welcome me, towering over us all and smiling as he did so.

"Hoe gaan dit," Willem Kotze said, not even making it a question, his smile slow and penetrating... almost *too* penetrating, as his gaze swept me from head to foot. "Ek is Viillll-haaaaam Kotze."

"Um... hi. I'm Sara... Sara Wright," I said, flustered, glancing over at Ana Marie. *Shame, man,* I wanted to say. *I know the word you were looking for —*

But Ana Marie wasn't even looking at me, all of her attention and angst directed towards her brother. "ENGLISH, you imbecile!," she practically shouted at him.

He said a few more words to her in Afrikaans as he walked towards us, prompting her to huff in exasperation, right as he turned to me with a flourish.

"Pardon... Sara." He leaned down and took my face in his hands, carefully, slowly, planting a kiss on each cheek, stroking my neck as he did so. "I shall have to work on my English a bit more," he whispered.

This kiss thing? Wasn't so unusual. Afrikaans men did it all the time at the church... of course, they were Afrikaans men in their eighties, and they sure didn't do it as sensually as Willem just had. And judging by the look on Ana Marie's face, I could guess that what he was doing wasn't entirely appropriate... as if I hadn't already gathered that simply based on how he was staring at me.

Call me crazy, though, but this just made me want to burst out laughing. Oh, I knew the English word for what Willem was — sexy. Shockingly so. I smiled over at Ana Marie, then looked back to Willem, who was smiling at me.

"Shame, man," I said to him. "I'm going to have to keep my eye on you."

"Perhaps you should keep them *both* on me," he replied confidently.

The night only continued to get more hilarious from that moment on for me. I'm sure the Bothas thought I was a complete lunatic, but as Willem spent the evening making open passes at me (much to his family's horror), I could hardly suppress the giggles. Oh, he was handsome enough, in a quirky sort of way, of course, but his greatest appeal was that he was oozing testosterone. Loads and loads of it. In his rugged, edgy way, he was probably the manliest man I had ever been around. Tall, dark, and big – in stature, personality, and manliness. I knew his type, and I praised God that his type had no effect on me, despite the way he smiled, as though he already had me in his bed.

Ana Marie mercifully sent the boys off to the other room after dinner, leaving the two of us to do the dishes alone. Riaan had gotten his mealtime reprieve from Willem's conversation and attention, and it had lightened his countenance. I had spent most of the meal, when I wasn't deflecting Boer advances, talking about our work at the center, about what God was doing through the Bothas, and the mere mention of how Christ had changed their lives seemed to soften the way Riaan looked at his brother-in-law…

… the brother-in-law who hardly seemed to hear anything because he was staring at me so intently. And rubbing my foot with his under the table. And at one point, even putting his hand on my knee.

He was good. And blatantly obvious about all of his flirtations.

"I'm sorry about Willem," Ana Marie hissed at me as she washed and I dried. "He's just… well, you know. That's Willem."

"He's hilarious," I whispered back. "I mean, he's so sexy he's practically a caricature of himself."

Ana Marie looked at me. "I don't know what that word means."

"Sexy?"

"No, shame, man, I KNOW what that means."

"Caricature?"

"Ja."

"It means he's almost like a cartoon character. So exaggerated and silly that the very things you hate about him are funny."

She studied me for a moment. "That makes him seem almost likeable."

"Well, maybe he is," I smiled. "Maybe God's brought him back here right now so that you can see the likeability in him, and maybe share Christ with him."

She frowned at me. "Shame, Sara!," she yelled.

"What?"

"Now, you've made this *all* about something bigger than me! Bigger than Riaan! And, now, I'm going to have to be nice to my brother."

I smiled. "It happens."


It was a late night that made for an early morning.

The morning came earlier than normal for me when, right at sunrise, someone began pounding on my front door.

I stumbled out of bed and to the door, groaning as I did so, only to peer through the peephole to find Daniel Boyd staring right back at me.

"For the love of –"

"Hey," he said simply, when I threw the door open. "You weren't asleep, were you?"

I stared at him blankly for a moment. "Of course, I was asleep. The sun isn't even up yet!"

"Sure it is," he said. "Or on its way up, at least." A pause. "Do you sleep in every morning?"

"This isn't sleeping in!"

He shrugged. "Well, whatever. Aren't you going to invite me in?"

I stepped aside, doubting the wisdom in doing anything but slamming the door in his face, given the hour and how annoyed I was to have been woken up so abruptly and for no apparent reason –

"So, you're probably wondering why I'm here," he said, in response to the thought I hadn't even verbalized.

"I was indeed," I sighed, crossing my arms over my chest and yawning.

"Business to take care of in Walvis Bay," he said simply. Thought I'd drive down early to be there when the government office opens so I can get away from the coast before the holiday towns wake up and all."

"Yeah, evil holiday towns with all of their *fun* and *happiness* and all the things you so easily detest," I muttered.

He stared back at me for a second… then slowly smiled. "Shame, man. You really *aren't* a morning person."

I rolled my eyes at him. "Well, early morning business in Walvis Bay doesn't explain why you're *here* in Swakop, and it certainly doesn't explain why you're here at my place."

He smiled, glancing around. "It looks nice. All that you've done since you moved in here."

I glanced around with him. "Thanks." Then, looking back at him, "Again, WHY are you here?"

"Thought I'd swing by here first, since it's on the way and all, and take you to breakfast. You know, 'team building' and all."

A pause. "For real?"

"Yeah, for real," he said, rolling his eyes. "I've only got an hour before I need to be back on the road, so are you ready?"

"I haven't even had time to –"

But I stopped myself from giving him the long list of all that I hadn't done to get ready for the day... and blew out a breath. What did it matter anyway? Not much, given the way he was already heading back to the door, clearly assuming that I was going to follow him.

"Sure. Let me go put on some shoes at least."


Fifteen minutes later, I was glad for the unasked for, unexpected wake up call.

As much as I knew about my holiday town, my knowledge paled in comparison to Daniel's, and the little restaurant he took me to was one that I had never even noticed before. Tucked away on a lonely little side street, lacking any real signage, and looking for all the world like nothing more than just a collection of empty rooms, it was a warm, inviting place specializing in enormous breakfast servings and bottomless coffee.

I hadn't eaten this well in months. And I was going about it with great enthusiasm.

"It's good to see a woman who isn't afraid to put away food like you're doing," Daniel observed, smiling at me.

This only gave me a moment's pause in my food shoveling... and then, I went right back to it. "Bacon," I said. "I haven't had bacon like this in a good, long while. How did you know about this place?"

He shrugged. "Just one of those things I've picked up on over the years."

"I thought you didn't know anything about Swakopmund," I said, taking another sip of coffee.

"I know a few things," he murmured, distracted for a moment by something across the room.

Just as I turned to see what the distraction was, Daniel stood to his feet abruptly and began walking towards a young man, likely just a teenager, who was making even longer strides towards us.

"Brother Daniel!," the young man shouted, smiling broadly, embracing Daniel as he reached him.

"Johannes," Daniel laughed, patting his back fondly. "Hoe gaan dit?"

"Baie goed," the teen laughed back. "I thought you were still in Windhoek."

"Ja," Daniel nodded. "Just down for the day."

"Well, I'm glad to have run into you, then," the young man laughed enthusiastically. Then, glancing at me, with an even broader grin, "Have you... have you married, Brother Daniel?"

I choked on my bacon just a little at the very thought, and –

"Naaaaaay, man," Daniel chortled out, glancing over at me. "This is Sara Wright, another missionary from the board. Sara, this is my friend, Johannes Mmumba."

"Pleased to meet you," I said, holding my hand out to him.

As he returned the greeting, Daniel pulled another chair up to the table and gestured for another cup of coffee to be brought to us. "It's good to see you again, friend. It's been too long. How are things?"

Johannes sat down with a sigh. "I'm blessed. So blessed. And you?"

"The same," Daniel smiled. "I've been wanting to talk to you, actually, so it's completely God's doing that you're here this morning."

"Is it? What were you needing to talk with me about?"

"I'm going up north soon, next month, and I'm thinking of doing some work along the border."

"Shame," Johannes sighed, leaning back in his chair. "It will still not be easy."

Daniel grinned. "Anything worth doing rarely is, friend."

"Yes, but there –"

"I remember, Johannes," he said softly.

Johannes looked over at me, concerned. Before I could ask about the apprehension in his eyes, Daniel sensed the question and began an explanation.

"Johannes is… or rather, was, a refugee from Angola, Sara."

"Oh," I breathed out softly, with no idea what this even meant. I knew so little of the history of this part of the world, likely so little of the history of those who I had come to minister alongside, and –

Daniel's smile acknowledged my ignorance. "His story," he said, glancing to his young friend, "is one that needs to be told to… well, to the world, actually."

"It was our story, Brother Daniel," Johannes said simply, "and the Lord's, of course."

"That it was," Daniel sighed. Then, looking at me, "Hearing it might just help you understand a bit more about some of the backgrounds of the people you're working with in the DRC."

"The DRC?," Johannes breathed out. "Is that where she's doing her work?"

"Ja, man," Daniel smiled. "And it's brilliant."

I was taken aback by this, seeing as how I had never heard him speak any kind or affirming words at all about what was going on in the DRC –

"Praise God for you, Miss Sara," Johannes said softly and sincerely.

Before I could respond to this, Daniel pushed his plate away. "Tell her your story, Johannes."

And so he did.

"When I was a boy, there was war," he began. "We never knew when there would be an attack, when things would be bad, and my mother knew this. She told me once that when the guns would fire, I was to hide myself. Under the bodies."

I fought back a gasp at this, swallowing unsteadily.

Johannes sighed. "And on the day that the gunfire came, as she said it would, the body that I hid underneath was hers." He paused for a moment. "I did not think it strange at the time, and I expected that she would wake again. When she did not, I made my way from body to body, hiding like she told me to. For a few days, I did this, moving and always watching and waiting for more gunfire, but it did not come. I was hungry and tired. And confused about what it all meant."

He looked down at his coffee. "There were missionaries. The few that remained, after the fighting began – they were there. And they snuck a bunch of us children into one of their bakkies and made their way across the border. It was dangerous, what they did, but they did so anyway. They spoke my language and soon, after we were across safely, they delivered us all to a man who did NOT speak our language." He smiled at this, shooting a glance at Daniel.

"Shame, man," Daniel smiled back. "I had only been on the field for a few weeks."

"Oh, I know," Johannes laughed. "And you were already in the big middle of this huge mess, likely not doing the job you were supposed to be doing. Right, Brother Daniel?"

Daniel shrugged. "Perhaps. But I got the call from the guy in Angola and figured the administrative stuff they had me doing even back then in the capitol could wait a while, especially since a load of children were heading right into the country and had no place to go."

"Yes," Johannes nodded, then looked at me. "Miss Sara, you must understand that we were all overwhelmed and scared. We had lost our parents, our homes, our very lives as we had known them... and then, there was this white man, greeting us all in his crazy foreign language, bringing us into a tiny mission house and feeding us more food than we had seen in a good, long while certainly. And as they made arrangements to find guardians for us, he began each day, to speak more and more of our language, just as we began to speak his."

"Just enough to tell you about Jesus, honestly," Daniel murmured.

"And what more important thing was there to tell, Brother Daniel?," Johannes smiled. "It was not hard to believe much about Jesus, God as man sent to save us from spiritual poverty, when God Himself had sent us a man to save us from earthly poverty."

"Hardly," Daniel sighed, seemingly uncomfortable with this praise. "I meant to have you tell her about what God did in your life. Not about what I did."

"Well, believe what you will about who you were to us," Johannes said, "but the conclusion I still come to, these many years later, is that God used it all for good. And He did many good things and is still, even today, doing many more. No matter what hardships and troubles we had, and there were many – God used them for good to bring us to faith in Him. And He used you, Brother Daniel... despite you, likely."

Daniel laughed out loud at this. "Well, I'll agree to that. Despite me. I could ask for nothing better than that, honestly."

I wondered at this, relishing the story they continued to tell about how Johannes and all of his companions had been found homes, how Daniel made it his mission, when it most certainly was not the board's mission for him, to make sure they all remained safe and healthy, sharing Christ and nurturing them in Him when he had opportunity.

And there it was. Another facet to an otherwise irritable and immensely frustrating Daniel Boyd. How many twists and turns and mysteries and –

Daniel caught me looking at him and raised his eyebrows, no doubt a snide comment ready to come from his lips, when Johannes stood.

"Shame, man, it was good to see you, but I have to go," he said, smiling and shaking our hands once again.

"Still early, friend," Daniel said, looking at his watch.

"Just in time for school, actually," Johannes said. "It is my last term, and I want to make sure to continue arriving on time."

"Best of luck," Daniel smiled at him. "Perhaps we'll see you again."

"I hope so, friend."

And with that, the joyful teenager made his way back out into the sleepy holiday town. For more than a few moments, I found myself unable to say anything at all, picturing the events from so many years ago, imagining Daniel with a whole bakkie load of refugee children, meeting practical needs and sharing Christ in a language he had to learn as he went. Incredible, even this, wondering at all that he had seen God do and witnessed firsthand –

"You would think," Daniel said softly, cutting into my thoughts, "that stories like his are exceptional. But so many people, especially where you're working, are just like that. Have stories just like that. Some even worse, because they didn't have the advantage of walking right into a good situation, after they left war."

A good situation, thanks to a good man, with unbelievably Good News, and —

"I should be getting on to Walvis Bay," Daniel said briskly, his mood already shifting. "Because that's why I'm here in Namibia, right? To do paperwork." He frowned at this.

I said nothing, thinking on all of these things. As we walked back to the flat, where his truck was parked and ready to take him on to the administrative tasks he had ahead, I briefed him, very quietly and around the lump in my throat, on all that was going on in our work at the center.

As we neared my front door and Daniel gave a small wave of dismissal, I bit my lip and considered the idiocy of what I was about to do.

And then I did it anyway, stepping near him and giving him a hug, no longer bothering to hold back my tears. I backed away as quickly as I had embraced him and, noting the dismayed and apprehensive look in his eyes, simply said, as the tears rolled down my face, "Thank you. For what you did for those children. You're a... a good man, Daniel."

And I wiped my tears, went back into my flat, and held my breath until I could hear him drive away.

The conversation with Johannes changed how I saw the DRC. It changed how I saw everything.

As we continued to work with the ladies, we were able to hear more of their stories, understand where they were coming from, and meet needs more efficiently. I was thankful for the changes, honestly, even if the stories the women told, the difficulties they shared with us, and their heartache they felt made it that much easier to cry, to feel, and to be even more connected to this place, wholly and completely.

Other changes were ones that I didn't welcome as readily. Willem's arrival had changed many things for me personally. The Bothas were still as involved with the center as they had been before, but most of their free time was now being taken up with Willem, adjusting to the changes in their home, and spending what time they could together alone now that they had a roommate who never gave them a moment's peace.

Unfortunately, it meant that I had more time than ever by myself. While Willem went out of his way every time I saw him to make it painfully clear that I could spend my evenings with him, I declined his advances and spent most of my time alone.

There were lonely nights, where I wondered at some points if anyone would notice if I just disappeared completely.

My mind went to Daniel on some of those nights, wondering what life was like in Windhoek.

And for some reason, I always ended up calling Jon.


To: Sara Wright (sarawright@gonowmissions.org)

From: Daniel Boyd (danielboyd@gonowmissions.org)

Subject: The Board

Sara,

The board has just informed me that they've just received your reports on the center. And, with that, they've informed me that you and I need to come up with some plans as to how YOUR work here in Namibia will change MY work here in Namibia. Because you are suddenly the golden goddess of missionary work here in Africa, and none of my education, experience, or expertise matters a whit in comparison to your Midas touch. Can I tell you, again, how much I LOVE the board?

But whatever. Nothing I can do to change things now, so we best be getting on with plans to present to them, detailing how we're going to change the world for Christ, using jewelry. Yes, jewelry. Because that makes such good sense, right?

Thoughts? Because I'm sure the board will love yours.

Daniel

Riaan, Ana Marie, and Willem had convinced me to go out with them.

"You are much too lonely up in the cold, dark flat," Ana Marie told me as she dragged me out. "And depressed! Why are you depressed?"

Well, I had plenty of reasons. Jon was calling literally every day, probably because I was leading him on, was leading myself on. And the irritated emails from Daniel, concluding in that afternoon's even more irritated phone call, where we had resolved nothing for the report that was due to the board that very evening, had done nothing to make the loneliness abate.

"I'm not depressed," I muttered. "Just... tired."

"You've been working too hard!," Ana Marie chided. "We've all been working too hard. Which is why tonight is *baie goed*, friend!" Then in a lower voice, "Shame, man, though, you must watch Willem's hands tonight, ne?"

"Willem's hands?," I asked, instantly wary. "Why would I need to –"

"Because I will not be able to convince him to be content with having just his sister, you see," she said. "I will give you Riaan when I can, but eventually? Willem will have none of it and will take you from him."

"What are you even talking about?," I asked, horrified by the worst case scenarios running through my mind, and –

"We're going *dancing*!"

Sure enough, two hours later, I had only managed one dance with sweet, kind, gentlemanly Riaan before loud, brash, bold Willem twirled me away from his brother-in-law's arms and into his…. where I had remained ever since. He was a great dancer, once we established an understanding about where his hands (and other body parts) were allowed and where they decidedly were *not* allowed. I found myself even smiling, the stresses of the work and the loneliness fading from my mind as Willem entertained me with his stories, in his lovely accent, and –

"I'm exhausted," I laughed out loud, pressing my hands to his chest. "Can we sit? Please?"

"Ja, ja," he answered, tucking my arm through his, leading me from the floor and to a table, where he motioned for two drinks to be brought to us. "You are a much better dancer than Ana Marie!," he exclaimed.

Ana Marie was just a few steps away from being a professional, as was Riaan. Even now they were amazing everyone else out on the dance floor. "I don't think so, friend," I said, grinning at him.

"Well, I much prefer watching you move at least, anyway," he said, winking at me.

"Shame, man," I sighed. I'd been fielding these kinds of comments all night.

Just as he opened his mouth to offer up another suggestive observation, I'm sure, my phone rang. I had given it to Willem to hold for me, since I had no pockets, and I was alarmed when he took it out, smiled broadly at me, and answered it.

"Sara's phone! Hoe gaan dit?," he shouted over the loud music.

He listened for a moment. "Ja, man, she's right here, looking sexy and – "

"Oh, good grief, Willem," I protested, reaching out to grab the phone from him, just as he moved away from me, grinning madly.

Another pause. "Is it? Ja…. ja. This is Villll-haaaam Kotze, you see," he said, exaggerating his accent, "Sara's lovey."

"Willem," I said, reaching across the table again, just as he grabbed my hands and held them in place.

"Shame, man… we are at a…. a… wat is dit in Engelse.. a… *bar*! Ja! I have taken Sara to a bar and shall take her back to my room later for more private fun if she will go for it, ne?"

And with that, I grabbed the phone from him, praying that it wasn't Daniel on the other end of the line, calling to apologize, and –

"Hello?"

A pause. An international call, then. Even better. "Who is Villll-haaaam?!"

Jon.

"Oh, someone very, very naughty," I said, glaring at Willem, who was now leaning back in his chair, smiling at the waitress who had brought our drinks.

"Naughty?," Jon sputtered.

"Not like that," I sighed. "Actually, probably just like that."

"Ja, man," Willem affirmed, grinning at me wickedly.

I pointed my finger at him in warning. "But not that I would know or have any intention of knowing. He's Ana Marie's brother."

Another pause. "Do you regularly go out to bars with him?"

"Not normally, but... well, I needed to get out tonight," I said, honestly. "And all of us have needed the break." A pause. "How are you, Jon?"

"Not too well, knowing that my girlfriend is hanging out in bars with questionable men."

"Girlfriend?," I asked, surprised by the term. "When did... we haven't... what?"

"Sara, I've been sitting here all day, waiting for you to call!"

Had I said I would call? Why had I forgotten this? And when had I fallen into the pattern of calling him so often, letting him call me so much, and –

"Jon, we talked last night. And every night this week, before that."

Nothing but silence for a moment. Then, a deep breath, half a world away. "Well, I enjoy talking to you. I miss you."

And while it was the moment to tell him that I missed him, too, I found myself unable to say the simple words. I was lonely, tired, and probably more than a little depressed, wondering how I fit into this place, but it wasn't Jon that I missed. It was feeling like I had somewhere I belonged. And maybe all he had been in this transition was just a way to feel like that.

"Sara? Are you still there?"

I sighed. "Yeah. I'm here. I'm sorry that I didn't call. I just... needed to get out. You know?"

He didn't, though. I could hear that he didn't understand. "Sara, I just want you to come home. You've had your time there, and now I think you should just come home to me, and –"

"Come home?," I said, talking over him, as Willem studied my face. Home sounded so nice some days, but what was happening here meant something. And it wasn't worth throwing out so simply, simply because it involved a few lonely nights. "This isn't just some vacation, Jon. This is my life now, and –"

"And I thought," Jon said, talking over me as well, "that you wanted some kind of future with me –"

"I... I thought I did. But I think my future is here. Even if it's... well... lonely. And sometimes depressing," I concluded. I glanced at Willem, who was making eyes at a woman across the room, even as he continued drinking and holding my hand on the table.

"Depressing? Lonely? Is it that bad?," Jon asked.

I shook my head. "Sometimes, but... that's life, right? I was depressed and lonely towards the end of our six years together, you know? And it... well, it didn't make a difference to you then. And I got through it. And I'll get through this."

"Are you ever going to let me live down my mistakes from back then?," he asked, exasperated.

I was so tired. "I just... don't want to talk about it right now. Okay?"

"Sara –"

"Goodbye, Jon."

And I hung up on him. It was too much, dealing with him when I wasn't sure I even wanted him anyway. Before I could feel guilty about it, before I could pick up the phone and call him back, I looked over to Willem.

He smiled and said, "Well. You told him!"

"That I did, huh?"

"Sara," he said, leaning forward meaningfully. "There is no need for you to be lonely when I am here, you know."

"Shame, Willem," I said. "I appreciate that, but... I think I'll get through it on my own."

"Are you sure?," he murmured.

"Ja, friend. I am."

A pause. "Then, would you mind if I go and speak with that young lady across the room?"

I smiled. "By all means, Willem. Please."


The Bothas dropped me off two hours later, but before I could collapse into my bed, my head swimming from all the noise and the exhaustion from the evening, my phone rang. Again.

"Oh, Jon," I groaned once I answered, "I really need some time, okay?"

"What?"

A sigh. "Daniel."

"You're coming with me to the north," he began, irritated, without any further pleasantries. Didn't he know I was up to my ears in work for the center?

"Hey, I'm super busy here," I started to explain to him. "I can't just –"

"Not my request," he said, a familiar shortness to his words. "I've been TOLD by the board that you're to go up north with me. Totally inappropriate as you are not a man –"

"Yes, yes, I'm not Mr. Shiftoka," I said, reminding him of what he had already told me ten thousand times since I had arrived here.

"Yes, and as you know NONE of the languages we'll need to know there, but who am I to tell the board anything about this country since they apparently know it all?"

I didn't say anything for a moment. "Were you looking for me to answer that?"

"Well, you do have all the answers, according to the board."

"Daniel, I don't want to go up north with you."

"Well," he breathed out, "I appreciate your honesty, at least. And I actually agree with your rather blunt implication that I'm bad company and all, but –"

"I didn't mean it that way –"

"*But*," he went on without waiting for me to finish, "the board hasn't given either of us a choice on this one. Cry me a river, Sara. We're stuck together on this one. That's just life."

I sighed. "Why have they suddenly made this decision?"

"They couldn't understand tonight, on our conference call, why I hadn't gone over any feasible ministry plans with you. And when I tried to use the distance between Windhoek and Swakopmund as an excuse, they told me that I needed to take you with me on my trip." A sigh. "And you know? The more I think about it, the more I think it's probably a decent idea. Apart from being, like I said, completely inappropriate and inconvenient and a waste of mission dollars."

A pause. "How is it a decent idea, then?"

"Well," he said tersely, "it'll be good for you to see what I do. And to see the rest of the country. You know, beyond the holiday town."

It would be very good. Honestly, I had spent more time than I cared to admit wondering about Daniel, about what he did, about what he was like on the field, away from administrative tasks, the board, and —

"I'll be there to pick you up tomorrow morning. Pack for six days."


To: Sara Wright (sarawright@gonowmissions.org)

From: Jonathan Parker (jbparker@americorp.com)

Subject: You

Sara, I'm sorry. I wish you would answer my calls. I didn't mean to be rude about your friend or about what you're doing there. I think you're doing a wonderful thing, spending this time in Africa. I just miss you.

Can I call you this week? Please?

Love you,

Jon

# 5 CHAPTER FIVE

It had been a long two days.

Daniel had picked me up at the crack of dawn in Swakopmund, and we had driven to Tsumeb, stopping only briefly there at the mission house to check on some maintenance issues. As we sped through most of the country, Daniel pointed things out to me, his mood lightening considerably the farther we got away from the holiday town. From Tsumeb, he pushed on to Oshakati where we only stayed for the night. Then, it was back in the bakkie and up as far north as we would go, over to Ruacana Falls.

We didn't actually see the falls on our drive in with our windows down in the dusty heat, though, as Daniel was determined to make camp for the night before the sun went down.

After he pulled in to a wooded, secluded area, I took a good look at myself as I jumped out of the truck to stretch. "Oh, geez, I'm filthy," I said to him, as I looked through my backpack for soap, shampoo, and everything I would need to get cleaned up. "Are there showers at the campground?"

"There are no showers, Sara." Daniel was so amused by my naivete that he allowed himself a smile.

"I thought you said we were making camp."

He nodded, his eyes never leaving his work. "Yeah. We are. Right here."

"We're in…" I looked around. "Well, the middle of nowhere! How is this camp?"

"You're not in America anymore. This is a great place to camp. You even have somewhere to get cleaned up."

"Where?"

He pointed towards the water. "The Kunene River. Though don't go too far — it's the border, and you don't want to wander into Angola and get… well, you know, get your legs blown off by a land mine or something."

I ignored this terrifying tidbit of information and looked at the water doubtfully. "That water's filthy, though… right?"

He shrugged as he continued to unload the bakkie. "Well, I wouldn't drink from it. But it's fine for rinsing off the grime."

"Fine for rinsing off the grime," I rhymed, weighing the cost of trying it out over potentially contracting some amoeba. "Where's the waterfall? I can hear it."

"Yeah, you're not going to go all the way down there. I'll take you tomorrow morning if you want to see it, but not tonight," he said. "Too many wild animals for you to go far from camp." He threw the last of the packs down and looked towards the water himself.

"Wild animals? Baboons, you mean?" I had seen enough of the baboons already, frankly. They were as domesticated as squirrels in the States and about ten times more terrifying.

"Those… and crocodiles, probably." Then, without warning, he kicked off his shoes and began to take off his shirt.

"Crocodiles?," I asked, weakly, all of my attention suddenly diverted to his amazing body.

"Yep," he said, walking towards the water, loosening his belt as he did so. Then, looking over his shoulder at me, he whispered, "Not that it makes any difference at all to me, of course, but you might want to turn around." He indicated his shorts.

"Oh!," I said, turning around. "Of course, of course."

I could hear his shorts hit the ground. "I'll be sure and give you the same courtesy," he said, "if you decide to brave the crocs as well."

And with that, there was a splash, as I forced myself to keep my eyes on my backpack, my face blazing.


The next morning, Daniel kept his promise and took me down to the falls.

The closer we got to the water, the harder it was to hear one another, until we were there, watching the water pound onto the rocks below, sending spray up all around, drowning out all other sounds. After watching for a few minutes, taking pictures as I smiled at the rainbows cast from the constant rushing, I looked over to Daniel, who motioned me towards a small hill. I climbed up behind him, matching his steps carefully on the slippery surfaces, reaching out and grabbing his shoulder at one point to steady myself.

"Thought you were trying to toss me over the falls back there," he said once we reached a clearing where we could see the water but could still hear one another. He pulled a jacket from his backpack as he smiled at me and laid it on the wet ground, motioning for me to take a seat next to him.

"No one would have ever known," I said. "Daniel Boyd, career missionary to Namibia, dead at the hands of Sara Wright, missionary sent to complicate all of his missional strategies."

"Hmm," he smiled. "That's an apt description."

"Of course, you'd think so," I said, snapping a picture of him.

"Stop that," he said.

I pointed my camera back towards the falls, snapping more and more. "There's a point to this, Daniel," I said. "These pictures make this place real for the people back in the US. They're more likely to give, to invest themselves emotionally into what's going on here if they can see it, can hear the stories, can almost feel what we feel, all the way across the Atlantic."

He looked at me dubiously. "Great in theory, I suppose."

"Great in reality," I replied, adjusting the lens. "I've raised enough money to cover all the expenses for the center for the next six months."

"For real?"

"For real." I smiled at him, then looked back over the falls. "Not costing you a thing, having me here."

"Hmm."

I rolled my eyes, unable to hide my smile at the troubled look on his face. "Are you bothered by that?"

"No. Not at all," he muttered, clearly bothered.

"Can I ask you a question?," I said, the very question burning in the back of my mind, just as it had these months since meeting him.

He looked at me suspiciously. "Well, if you must."

"How did you even end up here? In mission work? In Namibia?"

"Oh, that's easy," he sighed. "You want the short version or the long version?"

"I've got time," I put my camera in my lap and leaned back to look at him. "Give me the long version."

"King scorpion," he said.

"What?"

"Right there, by your foot," he said calmly, reaching his own foot out and kicking a scorpion the size of his hand away from me.

I clutched his arm when I saw it. "Oh, my –"

"Stings like... well, you can imagine," he said.

"Maybe I shouldn't be sitting here," I said, hugging my legs close to me, looking around where we were sitting.

"You're kind of squeamish, aren't you?"

I gave him a look. "Not as squeamish as you would think, but... yeah."

He shrugged. "Figures."

I took a deep breath, looking at him again. "You were going to tell me about how you ended up here, with various amounts of creepy crawly stinging bugs and –"

"And a squeamish woman," he nodded. "Well, I was in college and got roped into doing some volunteer work at a shelter downtown. Part of the requirement for some of the grants that were paying for my school." He looked over at me. "You probably didn't go to college on grants, did you?"

"No, my parents paid for it all," I said.

He nodded his head. "Yeah, well, this particular 'free' money came with hours of required work at this shelter. So, I was there doing my thing, and the guy in charge noticed that it didn't seem to mess me up when drunks were beating the snot out of one another and all kinds of dysfunction was exploding all around me."

"That sounds awful," I said.

"It was awful, but that's life," he shrugged. "Anyway, the guy in charge arranged for me to work at *another* shelter to help them out with some of the same issues they were having because I had all the time in the world, right? And that shelter was run by a church group, which was fine by me because I had nothing against Jesus."

"Nothing against Jesus," I smiled. "I like that."

He allowed himself a smile in my direction. "Yeah. Well, it was more than that. I already believed by that point. And was feeling a call to some type of ministry already. Totally not suit and a tie in the pulpit kind of ministry, though," he added, with a mild look of disgust on his face.

"Yeah, that's not you," I smiled, leaning my head on my knees as I watched him.

"Not at all. Anyway, the pastor there at the church was overworked and stressed out, clearly, but he had a real heart for this shelter ministry, and before long, we were running a really efficient operation, actually helping people to move past their issues, and making a difference. And so, I concluded that I was cut out for THIS kind of ministry, that working with people in these kinds of situations didn't exhaust me as much as it exhilarates me when frankly? People in most situations exhaust me."

"You don't say..."

He gave me a real smile. "I do say. And as I looked into it, kept working, kept up with school, I concluded that there were some real needs no matter where you go, that God is ready and willing to change lives and change the world. And the greatest needs? The places that people generally don't want to go to? Are overseas."

"And you ended up here... how?"

"Luck of the draw," he said. "Spun a globe, put my finger down, and landed on Namibia."

A pause. "Not really, right?"

"Well, not really," he sighed. "But close enough. There was a list of opportunities with the greatest needs – places without any missionaries. So, I went with this position, in one of those places. And as it turned out, it was a good fit. The languages here came pretty quickly to me."

"And so here you are," I said.

"And that's that."

"Well, that long version was surprisingly short."

"Should've heard the short version," he shrugged. "Come on, we've got a lot of kilometers to burn today."


Camping in Namibia? Was *really* camping.

There was no plumbing anywhere we went, it seemed, and running water was limited to what I got when I poured out one of the bottles Daniel had packed.

This was an issue, late at night in the pitch dark, when I found myself in need of a real bathroom. Or, failing that, just a bush or two to duck behind to preserve my modesty as I went.

As I set out, looking for just that in the middle of the night, I listened to make sure that I was alone. That wild, predatory animals, or worse yet, Daniel, weren't lurking in the dark somewhere, ready to give witness to what I couldn't believe I had been reduced to doing outside in the middle of the wilderness, and –

Oh, well. It was done, and I was well on my way back to my tent when I finally looked up and saw them.

The stars. All the stars.

I hadn't noticed them much in Fort Worth. And I hadn't noticed them even in San Juan. I had hardly taken the time to even look up at the sky in Swakopmund.

But here? I was struck by how many there were, how pristine and clear they were, and how… I had never even noticed.

Wasn't that true about so much in my life, though? I had certainly always believed the Gospel, had known its truth from as early as I could remember it, and had professed to follow Christ and honor Him with my life…

But what had that really looked like? Had I lived for Him, or had I reserved so much of myself, my ambitions, my dreams, and all my hopes for the future for myself?

I was different here. Different than I had been over a year ago, certainly. Even different than I had been in Costa Rica, where serving alongside so many others had been like an extension of my life in the States, fulfilling and fun, with plenty of friends and support to lean on. But here? I was so often left alone with Christ alone, being forced to trust in Him and no one else. And while I struggled with what that looked like, how I could deal with it, and the temptations of loneliness, I had seen the fruit it had borne, what relying on Him alone and being forced to trust Him only, had done in my life.

I wouldn't be the same. He wouldn't be the same to me.

And at this thought, I had to smile just a little. Frightening stuff, imagining that the rest of my life could be characterized by a desperate, tenacious grip on the sufficiency of Christ alone… empowering stuff, knowing that as I cowered and bowed in my own inadequacy, He walked before me, powerful and mighty and able to do all that I never could.

Different. All of it.

And this was more than okay with me.


Our days were spent meeting people in random, small places that weren't on the map. I wasn't sure how Daniel was able to find the locations at all and how he was able to even keep track of who was where or even our purpose in visiting people, sharing a drink or two, and sharing the Gospel.

Or, in my case, just listening while Daniel and a series of different, random men discussed deep spiritual mysteries in languages that I couldn't understand. Even my smattering of Afrikaans was little help this far north, and I sighed as we pulled into the middle of nowhere, literally at the end of the day with the intent of meeting up yet again with someone I wouldn't be able to understand. I opted to stay in the bakkie and managed a nap while Daniel went to chat for a couple of hours.

The squawking and clucking woke me up.

I sat up rather abruptly, wondering if the sounds were from some bizarre dream and gasped to see that they were all reality, as my eyes settled on Daniel, walking up to the bakkie with a live chicken in his hands.

"What is *that*?," I managed, horrified.

He gave me a long look. "A chicken."

"I know that, but why –"

"A gift," he said, holding it up as it continued flailing. "And a very generous one at that. One that I'm glad to get as I haven't had a decent meal since leaving Windhoek."

I recoiled at this slightly. "Are you going to... *eat* that chicken?"

"Nope," he said, opening the driver's door and climbing in, "*we* are going to eat this chicken."

"Don't bring it in here!," I shouted, moving away from him. "Do you want it to peck out your eyes?"

"No, I was planning on having you hold it for me," he said, attempting to pass it over to me as I began screaming and laughing, rather hysterically.

"No! No, no, no!"

"Ahh, geez," he rolled his eyes, not even attempting to hide his smile, as he climbed back out of the bakkie, the chicken still in his hand. "I knew you were squeamish, but –"

And he turned his back to me, stopping the squawking and clucking with a brisk movement.

I gasped. "Did you... *kill* it?"

"How are we going to eat it if I don't kill it?," he asked, smiling.

"But it..." I began, feeling irrationally upset by this. "It wasn't hurting anything."

"Then why were you screeching like that?," he said, very amused. "I was going to let it enjoy one last ride in the bakkie, but you were acting so crazy that I mercifully sent him on to glory a little early."

"Shame, man," I laughed. "I just... how are we going to *eat* that?"

He put the chicken in the back of the bakkie, climbed in, and shook his head at me, smiling. "We're going to do what our grandmothers likely did when they stepped right onto the farm, found their dinner clucking and kicking, and –"

"My grandmother went to the grocery store," I said, grinning at him.

He returned the smile. "Your grandmother was better off than mine, then."

"I don't even think my grandmother would have known what to do with a live chicken, and –"

"Well, then, you'll be more of a pioneer woman than she was after tonight," Daniel concluded.

Several hours, many screams of disgust, and even more laughs later, we ate dinner.

And just like everything else up north had been, it was incredible.


We spent the next day in a series of shebeens (which were, very frankly, dive bars), with Daniel alternately freaking out large groups of strangers then mesmerizing them with the stories he told. Unlike our holiday town, where Germans and Afrikaners were just as numerous as Owambos and Hereros, we were in a place now where white people were still an oddity. And Daniel was odder than most with his language skills, which were an endless source of fascination with the groups who would pull up chairs alongside us and would listen to the stories he told.

"What have you been telling them?," I asked, as one group in particular began animatedly discussing all that Daniel had been communicating, as we made our way to yet another shebeen.

"Just sharing the Gospel," he said succinctly. "It's baffling that the Lutheran missionaries came here hundreds of years ago and managed to make the people ritualistically religious yet completely neglected to communicate any lasting truth about grace." He looked at me. "Lutherans, mind you. Which is ironic."

"How is that ironic?," I asked, hustling to keep up with his brisk pace as he walked.

"Half the people in this country are named Martin because they're such great Lutherans. They should be the most reformed, grace by faith alone believers on the planet, but they don't have a clue. The missionaries worked hard on changing their behavior, their culture, who they were – things that, frankly, didn't need to be changed at all. And in the process, they missed out on the opportunity to share life-changing truths about Christ and grace. It's now missed so many generations. And we're left sharing who Christ is with people who think they know Him and honor Him by being religious, instead of just trusting Him and *really* knowing Him by faith."

He stopped abruptly and turned to me. And with great sincerity in his voice, he told me, "God forbid, Miss Wright, very literally, that we come and share grace on our terms and in our own thinking and play any part in deceiving these people by being a stumbling block to what God is already doing in their lives. God forbid that I make disciples twice as fit for hell as I would be myself, were it not for my redemption in Christ." He took a deep breath. "I need a beer."

I gave him a look. "You're an odd man, Daniel."

"How so?"

"You're saying all these profound things about these deep theological issues," I explained, "and then, you follow it up with... well, saying you need to drink."

"Nothing wrong with having a drink."

I didn't say anything.

He smiled at me. "You're making my point for me, Sara. Why do you think there's something wrong with having a drink?"

"Because it could lead you to drunkenness. Which, you know, IS a problem."

"Do I look drunk? After how many beers all over Owamboland?"

"No, which is troubling in and of itself," I said.

"Huh?," he asked, laughing out loud.

"It suggests a certain level of tolerance," I said. "Hard earned tolerance, likely."

"See? You're just making all kinds of crazy assumptions," he said, "based entirely on the presuppositions you're bringing to the situation."

"Pre... what?" He was making my head hurt.

"You assume, and likely because you've been told so in church, that it's wrong for me to have a drink. And because you assume so, you attribute to me all the negative things associated with drinking – that I have all this tolerance because I abuse the stuff, that I'm drunk, and that I'm some evil, villainous person for doing what I'm doing. Jesus didn't turn the water into grape juice, Sara. He turned it into alcohol. You only believe what you believe about it being wrong because you approach Scripture on the subject with the presupposition that it's wrong. And honestly? You're wrong on an issue that Scripture is pretty clear about anyway since Jesus Himself used wine to communicate some profound truths on redemption."

I frowned. "I grew up in a *good* church, where they wanted us to make *good* decisions –"

"I don't doubt it," he said. "But you grew up in a culturally *American* church. And that culture attributed some extra-biblical biases to their teachings to, in their thinking, protect people. But they told you something that wasn't scriptural. And they would likely snub their noses at Christ Himself if He came in their doors with wine in hand."

"Well," I huffed out.

"Well, indeed," he smiled. "The very same thing happened here, you know. Not about alcohol but about what real faith looks like. And those missionaries? Deceived people. They were well-intentioned, trying to help people as they thought best, but they were no better than Pharisees for what they did, attempting to make nice, little, proper German converts instead of true disciples of a limitless Christ. And you and I? Need to watch ourselves, so that as we share Christ we don't make the same mistake of forcing our own culture and biases on people, preventing them from truly receiving grace, which isn't bound by any culture. A pretty rudimentary missiological principle, actually, and one the board should have taught you before they sent you out here. But they were probably too busy going over how to fill out expense reports and spreadsheets because, hey, that's what they do stateside, right?"

A long pause as we watched one another.

"Well, now *I* need a drink," I said, very simply.

He laughed out loud at this, put his arm around my shoulders, and pulled me along with him towards the next shebeen.


We found ourselves, a day later, outside a corner store in Sesfontein, waiting on a man that was, by my estimation, three hours late.

It was hot. Painfully hot. And I felt my patience waning the longer we waited, feeling my skin start to burn underneath all the sweat.

"Maybe he's not coming, huh?," I asked, glancing around at the empty roads which hadn't seen any traffic in at least half an hour.

"He'll be here," Daniel said softly, patiently from where he laid on the ground, ankles crossed, sunglasses on, and his arms folded underneath his head, as though this was the most relaxing place in all the world.

Which perhaps it was... but the remoteness of the location, the sheer emptiness of the place, left me feeling a little edgy.

"Shame, man," I whispered. "He's late."

Daniel flipped his glasses up and looked at me. "He's right on time."

"Three hours late!," I exclaimed, looking at my watch.

"Exactly. Right on time."

I blew out a breath.

"Seriously, Sara," he said. "What else have we got to do but sit here and wait? We rob ourselves of real time back in the States when we become so obsessed with incremental time. You ever think the rest of the world has it right, being so laid back about it all, and we've got it wrong, being too caught up in it?"

"I think I would have brought some sunscreen if I'd known I'd be sitting out here in the sun for three hours... incrementally or otherwise."

He smiled at this. "There's some in the bakkie, if you want to grab it." He began standing up. "Actually, I'll be a gentleman and get it for you."

"Thanks."

I caught the bottle he tossed my direction a few moments later, squirted a liberal amount in my hands, and began spreading it on my face... pausing when a horrific odor floated towards my nose.

"Do you... smell that?," I asked, looking over at him.

He looked at me oddly. "No."

I sniffed my hands... and reeled at the rancid smell. "Holy cow!," I managed, rubbing my hands on my skirt frantically. "Are you sure this is sunscreen?!"

"Well, yeah," he said. "I've used it myself in the past."

"How long ago, though?"

"Oh, probably... the beginning of my term. So, ten years ago."

"Ugh! Do you *smell* it?!"

"Here," he said, putting his hand on the back of my neck and pulling my face up to his. "Oh, wow, that reeks."

"Thank you *so* much," I muttered... then gasping. "*Oh!* Now it's *burning!*"

"Burning?," he asked. "Well, the smell certainly indicates that maybe it went bad... not that I knew sunscreen *could* go bad, but –"

"*Ow, ow, ow!*," I began screeching, trying to wipe my face off on the bottom of my shirt.

"No need to get all indecent," he said, which was prompting enough to pull him right up next to me, where I began wiping my face on *his* shirt. "Oh, now you're going to get it on me!"

"Why did you even *give* me that stuff?!," I shrieked at him.

"I didn't know it would smell or burn like that, Sara," he said. "Honestly, it's just been sitting in the truck, and –"

"*Festering!* All those *years!*," I yelled, continuing to rub my face on his sleeve, still not getting it all off.

"Hold up," he sighed, prying my fingers off of his shirt and running to the bakkie, coming back with a bottle of water, which he promptly began to pour over my face. I would have gasped at the abruptness of it... but the relief from the burning kept me silent, as Daniel poured the water and brushed his fingers over my eyelids, my nose, my cheeks, my chin, my lips...

"There, better?," he asked softly, once it was all washed away.

I breathed out a sigh. "Yeah." I touched my face carefully... wondering at how it still felt hot to the touch. "Is it... do I have..." I wasn't even sure what to ask, but the expression on *his* face suggested that *my* face wasn't what it had been five minutes ago.

"Well, it –"

"Brother Daniel!"

We turned our eyes to the man walking up the road towards us.

"Ongaipi?," Daniel shouted out, to which the man grinned broadly and responded, "Nawa."

"Sara, this is Tobias Nujoma. Tobias, man, this is –"

Tobias couldn't hide his concern as his eyes drifted over my face. Oh, geez, what in the world did I –

"Sara Wright," Daniel continued, "Our new missionary to Swakop."

Tobias smiled. "Miss Sara, do you know that your face is –"

"Shame, man," Daniel said, laughing. "Let's talk church planting, ne?"

Two hours later, I was as clueless as I had been about what church planting up north looked like, thanks to the quick way Daniel and Tobias Nujoma switched from English for my benefit back to Oshiwambo for their own. How Daniel could seem to be more fluent in foreign languages than he was in his own was a mystery... as was what had happened to my face.

That mystery was resolved ten minutes after we parted ways with
Tobias and got into the bakkie, where I chanced a glance at my face in
Daniel's rearview mirror... only to discover red stripes from cheek to
cheek.

"What *happened*?!," I gasped. "Why are there *stripes* on my face?"

Daniel looked at me warily. "Well, I don't think you rubbed in the
sunscreen too well before it started... well, burning. Because those," he
said, taking my hand and putting it on my face, "match your fingers
perfectly."

It did. He was right. This didn't keep me from gasping again. "Look at
me! How long will it look like this?! Will I *always* have stripes on my
face?!"

He sighed. "That's a very vain thing to be concerned about, isn't it?"

I glowered at him. "Maybe so, but until *you're* the one looking like a
zebra, I don't think you can make that judgment of me."

"I'm sorry. Really."

"Yeah," I gave him a mocking laugh. "I can tell." Then, looking at my
face again, "Am I going to look hideous like this forever?"

"Sara," he said simply, "you're anything but hideous. Even with... well,
chemical burns, likely, you're still nothing short of beautiful."

I glanced over at him, surprised by this compliment, convicted by my
own pride that needed so desperately to hear it. Especially at that
moment, with my face in such a mess. "You know, I normally don't care
about the way I look, honestly... but I'll take what you said and believe it
for my own sanity. Thank you."

"You're welcome," he smiled, starting the bakkie and heading –

"Aren't we supposed to be going west?," I asked.

"Nope," he said. "We're heading back to Oshakati."

"Isn't that a little out of the way?," I asked. Understatement – it was the exact opposite direction that we were supposed to be heading.

"Yeah, but Tobias suggested it. Said that there are some seekers there, told me where to meet up with them." He glanced over at me. "So we will."

"Okay," I sighed, looking at my face again.

"And," he said, softly, "we're more likely to find something in Oshakati to help with your face. If you need something. Which, you know, I don't think you do."

"Thanks, Daniel," I said quietly. "I appreciate it."


Daniel had a history with so many people we met along the way. I told him on more than one occasion, as we stopped in at every shebeen and corner shop throughout Oshakati that next day and up into the places that had no names on any maps, that he must know every person in Namibia. "Just every Owambo," he said to me, as yet another crowd of young men approached him with smiles, hellos, and much laughter.

And just about every Himba, too, apparently, judging from the reception we received on the afternoon that we finally reached Opuwo.

My face had cleared up, which was a thrill. It had been an even bigger thrill, however, when Daniel told me that Opuwo would be a stop on our tour. He told me to pay special attention to the jewelry the women wore, as this might be a group that would benefit immensely from a ministry like the center's, especially since foreigners would be so interested in owning a piece of culture from this very secluded, very unreached people group.

What he neglected to tell me, however, was that the jewelry the Himba women wore was ALL that the Himba women wore. It didn't seem to shock anyone else as we entered the village that day, only me, as the women and children approached me with great wonder, putting their hands into my hair immediately, laughing to themselves and talking with great animation and amusement.

I looked at Daniel helplessly. "What's... what's the big fascination?"

"Blond hair," he said, leaving them to me as he made his way to the men, "they've never seen it."

The fascination ended for most a few moments later, with the exception of one toddler who threw his arms around me and wouldn't let go. His young mother was content to let him hang from my neck as I made my way over to Daniel, smiling down at the little guy as I approached the men. Daniel was speaking with the eldest man present in yet another language I had no idea he knew. Most of the eyes in the circle had been on me, with the exception of Daniel, who laughed out loud at something just said, prompting the other men to laugh as well.

I continued playing with my new small friend, sitting down in the dirt as other children came over to us, telling me so many stories and tales, none of which I had any way of understanding. I began singing Jesus Loves Me to them and was amazed by how quickly they picked up the simple words of the chorus and sang along, with much laughter and clapping. After a long while, the men stood, and the women called to their children, hurrying away from us.

"What's going on?," I asked Daniel, softly, watching as the whole place cleared out.

He sat next to me. "They want to honor us," he said. "Get ready to eat and dance."

"For real?," I smiled at him.

"For real."

We were three hours into the loud, wild party being thrown in our honor. A fire was blazing, and I had all but eaten myself into a sick stupor when Daniel pulled a long sleeved shirt out of his bag and handed it to me.

"Mosquitoes," he murmured to me, when I gave him a questioning look. "Last thing I need is to have to go stay in Swakopmund for a few weeks to help you recover from malaria. Cover up as best as you can."

I put his shirt on over my clothes and sighed when his scent hit my nose. "It smells like you," I murmured, before I could think better of it.

"Since I haven't had a decent shower in four days," he said, "I don't know whether to take that as a compliment or a rebuke."

"It smells good," I smiled, then gasped as he put his arm around my waist and pulled me right up next to him.

"Just play along," he whispered, as if anyone here could understand him anyway. "The chief here – don't look – seems to be under the impression that you're my woman." He raised his eyebrows at me.

"Your woman? And you didn't... correct his assumption?"

He shook his head. "Oh, no. I've known this guy for years, and he had no need for anything I've ever had to say beyond what medicine I can bring to his people until now, when I showed up with you. A woman with hair a color they've never even seen, frankly. I think they think you're some kind of angel... or demon maybe. I don't know. I'm a little fuzzy on the difference between the two terms in their language, honestly."

"Should have seen me with those red stripes on my face," I murmured. "Demon, indeed, right?"

"Absolutely."

"Well, did you tell them that I'm not —"

"Anyway, he's very impressed with me now that you're here," Daniel said over my protests. "You've suddenly given me great credibility in his eyes." He smiled the best smile I had perhaps ever seen him smile.

It charmed me completely. Which was likely his intent.

"Hmm…" I smiled, playing it up by putting my arms around his neck. "You're a lot more valuable now that you have a woman, huh? A demon woman at that."

"You bet," Daniel smiled back at me, sliding his other arm around me. "In fact, he's offered me two of his wives for you."

All merriment left my face. "Daniel Boyd, I —"

"Not an even trade, if you ask me. I mean, he's the chief, and I'm just a weird foreigner, right? What a disappointment for those two ladies."

"You —"

"I didn't take him up on it, even when he threw a whole bunch of cows into the mix," he said. "So, he thinks we're madly in love, I'm sure."

I sighed. "Well, that feels a little deceptive."

"Yeah, but he's going to let me tell everyone a little story here in a bit because of it," he smiled at me. "So, love me for the sake of the Gospel, okay?"

"If you say so," I said, tenderly kissing his cheek with great show, then snuggling up under his arm, as the circle grew quiet, and as Daniel, with great skill, began to tell them about Jesus in their very own language.

I had never experienced anything quite like that evening with the Himba. After loud and rowdy goodbyes, Daniel and I got back in the bakkie and headed towards...

"Where are we going?," I asked softly, with no idea what direction we were heading.

"Not really sure," he said. "Somewhere to camp. Can you tolerate it another night?"

"I don't suppose I have a choice," I said, yawning.

"Nope."

After a pause, I looked at him. "I've had a really great time. Doing this, you know."

He glanced over at me, a softness to his eyes. "Working?"

"Is this work?," I asked, smiling. "Going all over the country, meeting people, telling them about Jesus? How could this be work?"

He smiled. "I know. It's exhausting, but it doesn't feel like work." He sighed. "Now, when I get back to Windhoek and get back in touch with the real world, *then* it'll feel like work. Catching up on all those calls and emails and demands..."

"Shame, man," I said, pulling out my phone, "have you not been able to get phone reception out here?"

"No." He made a face at me, glancing at my phone. "Have you?"

"Uh, yeah," I said. "The whole trip, unfortunately."

"I can't believe you can get service out here," he said. "I mean, we're in... I don't even know where we are. I should've switched my own plan when I signed for yours."

"No, then *you* would have to deal with the real world right now, instead of having a reason to just ignore it," I said.

He thought about this for a moment. "True."

"I wish my coverage wasn't so great sometimes, so I could do the same thing."

"Want me to throw your phone out into the bush for you?," he asked, holding out his hand to do that very thing, grinning as he offered.

"Aww, Daniel, that's sweet of you, but I think I'd be regretting that once we get back to Swakop."

"Is that where your calls are coming from? Swakopmund?"

I sighed. "No, unfortunately, all... *twenty* of my missed calls are from the US. From the same person, actually."

"Missed calls? You're not picking up?"

"Nope."

He didn't say anything for a moment. "Are you worried there's some sort of emergency?"

"Oh, no, my parents would have called if that was the case."

"So..."

"So?"

"So, who are you avoiding?" He looked over at me. "None of my business, of course, but –"

"No, it's fine. I'm avoiding a gentleman by the name of Jonathan Parker. A very persistent gentleman."

"Apparently. Twenty calls seems pretty serious."

I sighed. "Well, it's a long story."

Daniel said nothing for a moment. "Well, I would tell you that we don't have time for a long story, but there's no time out here, you know," he said. "I mean, seriously. If you think time is irrelevant in Swakopmund, it doesn't even exist out here. You might as well take as long as you need. If you want to. Especially since I don't even know what direction I'm driving."

"That's so reassuring," I smiled over at him. "But, yeah. Jon and me. It's complicated."

He raised his eyebrows. "Ahh…"

"Yes," I said. "Just like that." I'm not sure why, but I felt free to just blurt out all my business here with Daniel, as we sat in the dark and the countryside flew by, right outside the windows. "We were together for six years. Which is a lifetime when you're in your twenties."

"Well, it is a long time," he said, looking over at me.

"Yeah, well, six years, then he was done. After I'd given him pretty much… well, everything I could." I bit my lip, thinking about this. "And I know it's all forgiven and all past, but… I can't help but hurt just a little when I think back to how much I trusted him and how he proved himself to be completely unworthy of any kind of trust."

"And… you're… with him now? Or something?," Daniel asked, puzzled, slowing his driving, pulling off on the side of the road, just in front of a clearing.

"No, I'm just… taking his calls. Letting him try to talk me into some kind of future." I turned to face him. "It's like the situation is reversed, you know? I mean, for years, I was the one pushing him, expecting things from him, and now, he's the one pushing me, expecting that I can commit to him, when… well, he's never given me any kind of indication that I can trust him."

"Do you still care about him? Like you did?"

I thought about this for a long while. The phone calls, the emails, the chats online... they were a good distraction from the loneliness that seemed to come sometimes. Jon was a reminder of home, of what it felt like to be known, and of what it meant to be desired by someone. At its very basest level, still being connected to Jon meant remembering that I was someone who couldn't be forgotten, even on the other side of the world.

But there wasn't much else there. Just a sad history that I had long since gotten over and was trying to move past.

"No. Not really," I finally admitted to myself. "I've changed a lot... I don't need him like I did before."

"Then why are you talking to him?"

"I don't know," I murmured. "Maybe because... it's lonely? Being here? And because... it's just hard, moving on from the past." I looked over at Daniel, thinking on the truth of this... and of the greater implications for the future, all that I was feeling, and the collection of moments treasured with him over this short amount of time.

How six years with Jon didn't even come close to how wonderful six days with Daniel had been.

"It's just hard," I said weakly, overwhelmed by what I was feeling for this strange, intense missionary who was now watching me, "letting go, even when you know doing so could open the door for something so much better."

Daniel, clueless to what I was going through, looked out at the darkness surrounding us and nodded his head. "It sure is," he said, his voice heavy, his mind on something he was keeping to himself.

We said nothing for a moment. "If it's any consolation, though," I murmured, "it's in knowing that I'm better off here, where I am now, doing what I'm doing now, than I would have been had things worked out differently with Jon."

"You think?," he asked.

"I know it... which, I guess should be my answer as to what to do regarding him, huh?"

Daniel shrugged, smiling slightly. "Could be."

"Shame, man," I sighed. "I'm sorry to dump this all on you, and... well, let me help you set up everything, okay?"

"You're okay, Sara," he said softly. "Let me take care of it tonight." And then, before he could say something else that was right there waiting to be said, he nodded his head, got out of the bakkie, and took care of it all.

We had reached the end of our six day trip and were headed back south, along the same dirt and gravel roads that had taken us up through all of Owamboland and into Opuwo. We had big plans for what could be done up north. Not just plans for what I could bring to the table but plans for what Daniel was already doing, how he could continue to further his work up here, and how all the relationships he had spent years building could yield many people won to Christ. The people loved him, and it was clear, every time we said good bye to another group, that they were going to sincerely miss him until the next time he could come again.

I was also going to miss him. I would miss seeing him every day, having grown accustomed in even this short time to waking up in my tent every morning to crawl out and find him already making breakfast over a fire, giving me a smile that couldn't be hidden by his scowl, as he said, "Well, you've finally decided to wake up, then, huh?"

I smiled even now as the sun rose over Namibia, sitting beside him in the truck, my mind running through such recent, sweet memories of all that we had seen and experienced together.

"Why are you smiling like that?," he asked, glancing at me out of the corner of his eye.

I sighed. "I just love this place."

He smiled at this. "I've gotta give you some credit. And I'm not in the habit of... well, handing out compliments, you know."

"I'm aware," I said, laughing a little.

"Yes, well," he sighed. "Then, you'll appreciate what I'm about to say even more. You, Sara Wright, have done very, very well on this little trip."

I looked at him, amused. "Well, thank you."

He shrugged. "Killing and cooking a chicken in the wilderness –"

"Well, you killed it."

"Oh, just let me credit that to you," he said.

"Okay."

"Surviving chemical burns on your face –"

"That was a big one," I affirmed.

"Yes," he agreed. "Pretending to be my woman –"

"More painful than the chemical burns," I laughed.

"I can imagine," he nodded, laughing with me.

"You forgot the wild dancing in Oshakati. Of course."

Daniel had gotten quite a laugh out of that episode, back in one of the more crowded shebeens up there, as he'd been encouraged by those around him who treated him like one of the family to get up and shake his stuff along with them. It had been hilarious to me, watching him really get into it, even as I wondered at how different this was – wild dancing in a bar – than what I had always assumed a missionary was supposed to do. But Daniel was all things to all people, remaining true to his convictions even as he sought ways to relate better to the people around him. He had pulled a very reluctant me up to dance with him as well, thinking better of it a few moments later when we were wrapped around one another, my flirty smile disappearing as his eyes locked on mine for a second or two longer than they probably should have.

Just thinking about it had my pulse fluttering all over again.

He smiled, his mind probably on the same things. "Yeah, I haven't forgotten that, Sara. And I'm pretty sure I won't ever forget it."

A quiet moment as my heart raced, as I'm sure I blushed –

"It's a shame that you've only seen a fraction of the country, you know," he said.

I shrugged. "Well, it was something. I'll have a chance to see everything else... eventually. Maybe." As I thought of the tight schedule we had ahead of us to have everything running and ready in time to coordinate with the churches I was working with stateside, I wondered if there would be any more chances at all. Life was getting very busy. I was pretty sure I couldn't spare even a few extra hours.

"I don't suppose," Daniel said, "that you can spare another day, huh?"

I looked over at him and very nearly forgot all that was pressing on me back in Swakopmund. "Another day? Why?"

"Well, there's one more place you should probably see while you're up here," he said. "They have showers. And real cabins. And every kind of animal that lives in Namibia." He looked at me. "Has any of that piqued your interest?"

"You had me at showers!," I exclaimed, bringing a smile to his face. "Where to?"

"Etosha."

A few hours later, we were there at Namibia's national game park, parting ways to go to our cabins to finally get properly cleaned up.

Before I could get to it, though, my phone buzzed at me. Make that now twenty-four calls from Jon.

I had to deal with this. I couldn't keep taking his calls, or *not* taking his calls, as the case was –

"Sara!," he practically shouted when I finally answered.

"Jon," I said softly.

"I've missed you! Are you okay?"

"I've been fine," I said. "Just traveling for work."

"Traveling? Geez, I've been so worried!"

"I should have let you know I'd be away. I'm sorry," I replied.

"No, I'm sorry, Sara, I'm so sorry for all that I said, and I didn't mean any of it, okay?"

"Jon," I began.

"No, I'm glad you're in Africa, doing what you're doing. Honestly."

"No," I said simply. "You're not."

A pause. "What?"

"You're not glad about it. This isn't... what you want."

A long silence, as Jon no doubt weighed the risk of telling me the truth.

"Okay, so it isn't," he breathed out. "I want you to be here with me."

I thought about all the days that I had wanted nothing more than to just be with him. And I thought about what life was now, how even with the difficulties, the hardships, and the challenges... how I wanted nothing more than to be where I was now, even if it meant being alone.

"We had six years," I said, thinking on just what this meant. Six years.

"Yes, and I messed it all up, Sara, I know," he sighed. "When are we going to get past the six years and how I messed it up?"

The truth was that we would likely never get over it. I would always remember. And what was more, it had *only* been six years, then it was over. And this? What we had been doing? Had done nothing to change my feelings.

We had changed. Both of us had changed. And we hadn't changed together.

And that was okay.

"Sara?"

"I think... I think we're really done, Jon."

A pause. "Because of what I said?"

"No," I sighed. "Because it was done a long time ago. And I think I was wrong to try and let this turn into something again because... I don't' think we want the same things anymore."

A long pause. "Sara, you need to think about this. I mean, you need to *really* think about this. Because saying goodbye now? Will mean goodbye forever."

I knew. And I was glad for the finality. "I have. I'm sorry, Jon."

After I hung up, I made my way numbly to the shower. And as I let the water pour over me, I thought about those six years, the time since, and all that Jon had meant in my life, expecting the tears to come, for all the years lost, for this final goodbye, and for the lonely nights that were up ahead.

And I was surprised to find that I had no tears to cry for him anymore.

"That," I told Daniel dramatically, when I finally emerged from my cabin, my hair still wet from the shower and my skin so clean it was tingling, "was awesome." There was more than one meaning to my statement, but Daniel didn't know the half of it as he grinned at me.

He patted the seat next to where he sat, watching the watering hole right outside my front door. "I was beginning to think you had washed down the drain. Took me half the time it took you."

"It was too wonderful to rush," I sighed.

He nodded. "The things we take for granted, you know?"

"No kidding," I muttered, settling in beside him, even as my phone buzzed at me.

"Jon?"

Though I had concluded to myself that the easy break had nothing to do with Daniel and everything to do with what I had already resolved in my own heart... I doubted that as I looked over at him and felt my heart race again.

"Um, actually," I said to him, "I've already talked with Jon once today."

"Ahh," he said, looking out over the watering hole as the elephants gathered there threw dust in the air with their trunks.

"I told him I'm done."

He looked at me. "Are you?"

I thought about this for a moment. "I think I've been done for a while." I looked at him. "And that's okay."

He nodded. "Well, good." A pause. "Who's calling now, though?," he said with a smile.

"Well, let's see," I said, looking at it. Willem Kotze. "Oh, someone else."

"How many men do you have calling you?," he asked with a laugh.

"I have no men, Daniel," I smiled, knowing that a blush rose on my face as I said it. "None."

Another pause as we watched the watering hole.

"Well, good," he concluded.


After a few hours of riding in his truck, trying to find the different animals all along the trail, I convinced Daniel to finally let me cook something for us, using most of what was left from the food we had already carried halfway across the country.

As we sat on the couch in my cabin afterwards, laughing about some of the funnier moments from our trip together, my phone buzzed. Again.

"Another man?," Daniel laughed, grabbing the phone from me, despite my protests.

"It's a text," I said. "Probably from Ana Marie, asking why you've stolen me for an extra day."

"Has it been that great of a trial, Sara?," he said, scrolling through my phone with a faint smile on his face.

"Not a trial at all," I said. "I just imagine my friends are wondering about me."

He nodded. "As is… Jon."

"So, what does his text say?," I said, leaning over his shoulder.

He handed me the phone. "I'm not going to read it. It's none of my business."

I took the phone from him, nodding. Then, after reading what Jon had written, I murmured, "Hmm."

Daniel said nothing for a minute. I turned the phone off and looked at him.

"So…"

"So?," I asked.

A pause. "What did it say?"

"None of your business, right?," I smiled at his curiosity.

He nodded. "None whatsoever… but still. You could tell me if you wanted to."

Another moment. "And why exactly would you care to know?"

"Well… I don't." He shrugged, crossing his arms over his chest, feigning indifference.

"Shame, man, if you want to know –"

"Okay, fine, so I do," he muttered with a small grin. "What did he say? You know, so I can be fully up to date on the emotional status of the only other member of the Namibian mission team."

"Ahh, so it's purely professional, then? This interest of yours?" I didn't wait for a response, wondering at my own boldness in saying even this. "He said that even though it's over, even though we're moving on… we can never be that far apart in reality because we're sleeping under the very same stars."

"Really?," Daniel asked dubiously.

"Yes, really. That's what he said."

He stared at me blankly for a moment.

"What?," I asked.

"That kind of cheesy talk works on you?"

"It's not cheesy," I said, punching his arm lightly. "It's a very nice sentiment."

"A nice sentiment," he smiled at me.

"Yes," I said, unable to stop from laughing. "Daniel..."

"It's completely cheesy, Sara," he laughed.

"Okay, so it's bad," I laughed with him, then gasped. "Shame, man, I don't want to laugh. He was my life for a long, long while. And cheesy sentiments like this?" I indicated my phone. "Worked ALL the time. Got me to... well, to do a lot of things I shouldn't have done." I put my phone on the couch between us, not meeting his eyes.

"Well, he's an idiot," Daniel said, very simply.

"What?," I asked, glancing up.

"You heard me," he said, looking at me very seriously, surprising compassion there in his eyes. "And not just because he let you get away before. And I don't want to laugh at him either because being him right now? Having lost you forever? Must truly, truly suck."

"Dankie, friend," I smiled. Then a pause, as I desperately wanted to ask him...

"What?," he said, smiling.

"Well… tell me the other reason he's an idiot," I laughed.

"Well," Daniel said, with great amusement, "he's an idiot because you're *not* sleeping under the very same stars."

I didn't get it. "What?"

"Southern hemisphere, Sara," he smiled. "Different stars."

"Are you for real?"

He laughed. "Yeah." Then, taking my hand in his, he led me to the door and stepped outside.

"Shame, man," I said, indicating his short sleeve shirt, "what about all the mosquitoes? Malaria and all that?"

"Those mosquitoes wouldn't dare bite me," he grinned. "I'm all bitter and sour, likely."

"True enough," I smiled at this.

"Besides, I've had malaria before. More than once. And after those intense periods of fever-induced hell on earth, I'm pretty much immune."

I couldn't imagine. "Who took care of you while you were sick?"

"No one," he said, smiling. "I suffered it out alone, crying all man-like and such until the fever broke and I stopped puking up everything I'd ever eaten."

"Then why," I said, "if you can suffer it alone did you tell me you'd have to come out to Swakop if I caught it?"

He didn't say anything for a moment. Then, softly, "I wouldn't want you to be sick like that by yourself. Not if I could do anything to help, you know."

"Thanks, Daniel," I murmured, as I leaned against his shoulder, his hand still holding mine, my eyes following his gaze up to the sky… where I couldn't see a single star. "So… where are these different stars that you told me about, hmm?"

"Well, that figures," he groaned. "It's all overcast. But I swear to you, on a clear night, you can see that all the constellations? Are totally different down here than they are back in the States."

"Really?"

"Yeah. So, when Jon," he said softly, "told you that you were sleeping under *his* stars, he was wrong. Because you've been sleeping under mine."

"Yours? Do they belong to you?"

"No," Daniel said, smiling. "They belong to us. And I'll show them to you. One day. I promise."

I sighed. "I'll hold you to it."


To: Sara Wright (sarawright@gonowmissions.org)

From: Melissa Thibideaux (mthibideaux@mail.com)

Subject: WHAT?!

Sara,

Okay, what in the hee-haw is going on?! Last I heard from you, you were living your African life with no drama, no men, and no complications, and now? To quote you, "I've ended things with Jon, and I think I'm love with Daniel."

Whoa, whoa, whoa. First of all, Jon?! Jon Parker? When did HE get back in the picture? And what do you mean you've ended things with him? When did you START things with him, AGAIN? I can't figure out why you wouldn't tell me any of this unless, oh, I don't know, you were afraid I would have said something like this – this is a bad, bad, bad idea, Sara. Which, guess what? I'm saying now, belatedly. That was a bad, bad, bad idea, Sara!

And Daniel?! Didn't you just tell me a few months ago that he was a complete lunatic and that you couldn't stand the sight of him?

You've got a lot of explaining to do. And if you don't do it quickly, you may find me on your doorstep. Because someone needs to go halfway around the world and kick some sense into you, girl!

Love you. No, really, I do. Now, EXPLAIN yourself!

Mel

# 6 CHAPTER SIX

I wasn't home even an hour when I got a call from Willem.

Ugh. More propositions, more drama, more than I wanted. After such an incredible week with Daniel, I was hesitant to jump back into it all.

But I called him back. Because the love of Christ, which is all the love I could muster for this guy at the moment, compelled me to do so... even if I did so with gritted teeth.

"Sara, lovey," he said to me. "We've missed you around here."

"Work, Willem, work," I said. "I had to go up north with my... well, my boss." Was that what Daniel was? Technically?

"Up north?"

"Yes, to Owamboland. Over to Opuwo. All of that."

He gave a laugh. "Sara, if you wanted to go see all of *that*, I could have flown you up there myself."

"Well, I appreciate that," I said. "But really, it was a week-long trip. And it was better to drive." A pause. "Why all the messages? What's going on?"

"I'm calling because I have to know… what have you done to my sister?"

And so followed a conversation about how Ana Marie was not like Ana Marie, how this whole born again thing had changed her, and how even Riaan was not as bitter and angry as he had been, back when the rift between him and Willem had started.

"They're being so kind!," he bellowed at me. "And I have not had much kindness in my life as of late, Sara. It is *very* unsettling. I must know why they are the way they are."

I took a deep breath. "Well, then, perhaps you should ask them about Jesus."

A pause. "I'm sorry. What?"

"Ask Riaan, friend," I said. "He can explain it without a translation."

And with a quick prayer said, I hung up the phone.

I was hard at work at the center the next day when Willem showed up.

Ana Marie had gone with Riaan to the DRC to transport the ladies back after a morning and afternoon of jewelry making. We were halfway through our most recent order, and I was excited about recruiting even more women on the next go round, knowing that we would have more opportunities to share the Gospel and provide income for them. It had been surprising to see how well everything had come together, with just a little help from the Bothas.

What wasn't so surprising was Willem's concerned expression when he bellowed into the center in his loud, heavy way.

"Sara!," he practically shouted. "I must speak with you!"

"We spoke yesterday, friend," I said, continuing to bag up extra materials. "And I suppose you spoke with Riaan afterwards, like I suggested."

"Ja," he nodded.

"So, you've done a lot of speaking already," I concluded, glancing up at him. "What is it now?"

"Are you annoyed with me, Sara?," he asked, a hurt look in his eyes.

I sighed, chiding myself for my impatience. "No, Willem," I said softly. "I'm just very busy. And very tired. It was a long week up north."

"Well," he said, still looking quite concerned and perplexed, "I won't take up much time. May we chat?"

"We *are* chatting," I said, pulling up a chair and indicating another to him.

But he was too busy pacing to sit still.

"So, I talked to Riaan about… Jesus. Like you said to."

"And?"

"And," he continued, "he said a lot of things that I have *never* heard, Sara!"

"Such as?"

"Well, you must understand," he said, "I was born and raised Dutch Reformed, ne?"

Yes, like most Afrikaans people. Baptized as infants, so that they could be married and buried by the national church. Jesus didn't have much to do with it, honestly.

"And," he kept on, not waiting for a response, "they never *told* me these things!"

"Willem, did you even go to church so that they *could* tell you these things?"

He thought about this for a moment. "Well… no. But I am baptized Dutch Reformed, Sara! I belong to the church!"

"It doesn't matter what church you belong to, friend, if you don't belong to Jesus."

"*That*," he yelled, "is exactly what *Riaan* said!" A pause. "Shaaaaaame, man. And you know that Riaan had no church before any of this Jesus business, so I thought he didn't know *what* he was even talking about… until he talked about the blood."

"The blood?," I asked, tilting my head curiously at this. "What blood?"

Willem plopped down in the seat across from me. Finally. "He said that every bad thing I have done is like a drop of blood. A drop of blood on a clean shirt, Sara. That I have to wear around, showing the whole world just how bad I am, ne?"

"Uh… well, yes, something like that. It's called sin."

"*Sin!*," Willem yelled. "Just like *Riaan* said!"

I nodded. "Yes."

"And I'm thinking…. sho, man. My shirt is one bloody mess. I mean, literally. A bloody mess." He considered this for a moment.

"Well, we all have more sins than we can likely count," I offered.

"Ja, except for Jesus, man," he said. "Riaan explained that Jesus had *no* sins. But that He took *my* dirty shirt, by spilling His own blood on the cross, and *took* it for *me*! And gave me a clean shirt in its place!" He backed away with an incredulous look, gesturing wildly with his hands. "Can you believe that?"

I smiled at this. "He did. And I can."

He paused for a moment, leaning forward. "I am a bad man, Sara," he said, matter-of-factly. "I have not had much need for goodness and decency. And I've spent most of my time stealing and cheating in business and in life."

"And how did that work out for you?," I asked, wondering at this.

"For a while, things were good," he said softly. "I was taking money from the company I worked for. Skimming a little off the top here and there, building up my own wealth at the expense of the business, taking clients on my own, and doing all that I could to look out for myself and no one else."

"Plenty of people are like that," I said. "And most of us are probably like that when it comes to how we view ourselves – as most important of all."

"Ja, and you know that kind of thinking and living catches up with you," he sighed. "Caught up with me, because I couldn't leave it at business alone, ne? Not only was I stealing money from the boss, but I stole his wife, too."

I watched him for a moment. "Is that what happened? In Cape Town? Why you had to come here?"

"Ja," he said. "Nowhere to go but to Riaan and Ana Marie. I knew Riaan would let me work for him, if only for her sake."

"And the company you left behind? Your boss... and his wife?"

"It was a mess. I'm not proud of it, Sara," he said softly, looking at me. "And while I thought I had reason, while she thought she had reason as well, we were wrong, and it caught up to us. The boss caught me with my pants down."

"So to speak," I said.

"Pardon?"

"With my pants down – metaphorically speaking, right?"

He looked confused. "What? What does that mean?"

"It's a saying in American English – 'with my pants down'— that doesn't literally mean 'with my pants down.' It means that you got caught unaware."

"Oh, ja," he nodded. "That I did. And my pants were actually *down*, Sara."

"Oh," I managed.

He gave me a funny look, with his quirky smile. "You Americans are crazy for having a phrase like that, you know?"

"Our language imitates real life... apparently," I smiled back.

"Ja, well, it was *real*, but... I've been feeling guilty about it. And now, to hear Riaan say that even these things I've done, so recently, that... well that Jesus can bear the weight of that as well..." He looked up at me with wonder in his eyes. "It is good news, ne?"

"The best, Willem," I smiled at him. "News worth living for, I would say."


I was more than a little mystified by the change in Willem.

Riaan and Ana Marie had come to faith as you would likely expect – with careful consideration, with some amount of reservation, and with a tentative approach to service and ministry. Willem, on the other hand, flew headfirst into it, holding nothing back and overwhelming us with his exuberance. He had taken my advice that very same day and had told Riaan that he'd given his life to Christ. I had expected the shock that this caused Riaan, but I could never have guessed at Willem's whole-hearted acceptance of the truth of Scripture. The witness of his sister, who had refrained from wringing his neck all these weeks that he'd been living in her home, had done its part, along with the Spirit's work of convicting his heart.

He was a changed man.

"Ag, man!," he shouted the day after praying with Riaan, as we made our way out to the DRC. "I should like to speak with the men there, if it is no problem with Sara." He shot me his winning smile, which was somehow far less seductive than it had been just a few days earlier.

"Uh... well, sure, I guess," I said cautiously. "Although we don't really have a lot going on with the men."

"Not yet," Willem laughed out loud, pounding his fist into Riaan's shoulder gleefully, causing his brother-in-law to nearly wreck the car. The two began exchanging very loud words with one another, Willem laughing and Riaan getting more and more irritated.

Ana Marie looked over at me. "Willem is... well, very excited. And Riaan is telling him that... well, I do not know the words in English. But I assume they are quite... um..."

"Vulgar? Rude? Explicit?," I offered.

"Ja," Ana Marie nodded simply. "He shall have to wash his mouth out with soap when we get home."

Thankfully, the car ride ended a moment later with our entrance into the DRC. We always had a plan in place, with the food we brought, the medicine, and all of the other ways we helped out the ladies and the families that we had been ministering to, and our plans never veered off task, for fear of creating pandemonium and hysteria in this sometimes volatile environment.

Riaan, Ana Marie, and I got out and moved to start working just as we always did… and were alarmed and concerned when Willem leapt on top of Riaan's car (much to his chagrin, I might add) and began yelling at the top of his lungs.

"Oh, Lord," I mumbled, already praying, even though I had no idea what he was saying. Ana Marie gasped, and Riaan went to try to pull him off the car, all to no avail, as throngs of people began to crowd around the car, pointing and smiling at Willem.

"What's he saying? Guys, what's he *saying*?!," I nearly shouted at them.

"He is," Riaan began, exasperated, "telling them all to come – the men, that is – to come and hear about what Jesus has done for him."

"Oh, well, that doesn't sound too bad, I guess –"

"And now he's telling them just exactly what kind of man he was before the Lord changed him, and…" A pause, as the crowd gathering around the car was growing quieter and quieter by the moment. "Oh, Sara," Riaan breathed. "I should very much *not* want to translate this for you, as it is…." He looked to me, red-faced.

"A bad story indeed," Ana Marie added. "Ag, man, shame, Willem! Have you no sense?!"

Willem continued on detailing his life of exploits and deceits with no evidence of stopping his tale, so I encouraged the Bothas to keep to the plan. And as we worked on all that we had determined to do that day in the DRC, Willem continued sharing his testimony, loudly and with great enthusiasm, much to the amusement and astonishment of the nearly one hundred people who had gathered to hear what the crazy, big Afrikaner had to say.

He only began to wrap things up just as we finished all of our own work, making plans for the week with the ladies who were going to be at the center. We stood and watched him, as many men continued to listen to him, visibly affected by his words.

But not as affected as Ana Marie, who began wiping away tears as Willem lowered his voice and said something very succinctly, his own words trembling with emotion.

I looked to Riaan for an explanation.

"He said," Riaan spoke with great gentleness, "that the grace of God is not something to be earned. For if it were, we should all be as... as, um, poor?" He looked to me for confirmation.

"Destitute, perhaps?"

"Ja, destitute as the worst of sinners, which Willem has said that he is." Riaan looked back at Willem. "And that grace that is given so freely and cannot be earned is something worth dying for... and all the more worth living for."

I didn't say anything for a moment as Willem leapt back off the car and went to speak personally with a few of the men who reached out for his hand and immediately began asking him questions.

"Amen," Ana Marie breathed through her tears, then looked to me, and began laughing joyfully.


The board arranged for Daniel to come out to the coast after they heard about how well the center and now our booming ministry to men in the DRC was doing. This was an irritation to him, as it changed his plans for some church planting work down in Luderitz, and he didn't hesitate to tell me, over the phone, how frustrated he was that he would have to spend the entire weekend "on holiday" in Swakopmund.

I wasn't much looking forward to welcoming his attitude to town either. But, oh, how I had missed him even with his attitude.

Since I had been home from the north, I had found myself thinking about him more and more often. Just as we had shared before, life was lonely, even with a handful of truly wonderful friends, a great church, and so much work to keep me busy. Coming home alone at night to a silent flat where I wouldn't speak to anyone again until the next time I reached out to make contact with someone else still left me feeling a bit adrift at times. I was surprised, though, to find that I wasn't just lonely for anyone... I was lonely for Daniel and his slow, infrequent smiles, even if they came with a brooding, moody demeanor at times.

I was pleased and surprised, then, when he showed up that Friday and seemed to have left his bad attitude in Windhoek. Riaan and Ana Marie had arranged to spend the day with us and finally meet Daniel as I planned to take him into the DRC and to the center on my side of town to show him the progress made since he had last visited. As we finally caught a glimpse of him walking towards the meeting spot we had settled on by the seawall, Ana Marie gasped, grabbed my hand, and whispered, "Ag, man! *That's* Daniel?!"

"Yes, that's him," I said, smiling to see him again. Then, shaking myself out of my stare, "Why?"

"Well, he's painfully *hot*," she nearly exclaimed, which earned her a scolding look from her husband. "I'm *wed*, Riaan, not *dead*."

"Clever," I told her, "the whole rhyme and all."

"Ja, I know," she giggled at me. "My English is hectic now that I have such a good American friend to speak with all the time."

I was about to tell her that she wasn't exactly using "hectic" the right way, but by then, Daniel was there with us. And after quick introductions, we showed him what had been done.


"And then," Riaan explained to Daniel, as we sat and discussed our strategies over lunch, "we have opportunity to take our tourist clients who are going up north over to the DRC, to meet the people, to see what's going on, and to bring them back here, to the center, to see and invest in what God is doing here. It's an opportunity to advance what the ladies are doing *and* an opportunity to share Christ with tourists."

Daniel considered this for a moment. "People... *want* to see the DRC?"

"Ja," Ana Marie smiled. "People, Daniel, even people who aren't born again, want to help with poverty. Even tourists. So we're giving them that opportunity and sharing Christ with them as we do it. They support our ladies, and our ladies share their faith with them."

Daniel looked over at me, smiling when I shrugged at him. "Well. That's so obvious that I'm amazed I didn't –"

"Goeie middag, hoe gaan dit," Willem breezed into the restaurant, winking at his sister as he scooted in next to me, practically pushing Daniel out of the way as he did so. "Sara," he said, not even bothering to look around the table, "I brought you more Super Cs."

I had told Willem offhandedly weeks ago that this was my favorite candy, even though I couldn't find the right flavor here in Swakopmund. Since then, he made it his goal on every flight up north to locate the right kind and bring it home to me. "Mmm... strawberry?," I said hopefully, holding out my hand to him.

"Strawberry-banana, even better," he smiled, dropping the rolls into my hand.

"Baie dankie, Willem, it is," I smiled, as he took my face in his hands and kissed me on my cheeks. "I'm keeping that shop up north where you find these in business, huh?"

"Ja, man, I know," he said. Then, noticing Daniel, "Goeie middag... who are you?"

Daniel was staring at all of us with unbridled shock. He came to quickly, though, holding his hand out to Willem, who took it. "Daniel."

Willem continued holding his hand. "Another American, ne? Are you Sara's... brother?"

"I don't have a brother," I said. "Daniel is my boss."

Daniel and Willem continued squeezing one another's hands... tightly enough that I could see the veins becoming more pronounced in their wrists.

"More of her teammate than her boss, actually," Daniel managed.

"So you make pretty little bracelets, too?," Willem smiled.

Before Daniel could come completely unglued (and judging by the look on his face, he was close), Riaan spoke up. "Daniel, this is Ana Marie's brother, Willem. He just became a believer."

Willem let go of Daniel's hand, smiling as he did so. "Ja, man. Thought the whole lot of them were crazy, honestly, but seems they're not." He looked around at us. "So, are we going to the DRC this afternoon, like normal?"

"What in the world was that?," Daniel whispered to me after lunch, leaning his head close to mine as he linked my arm through his and walked me to his truck. We had said goodbye to the Bothas and to Willem, the latter of whom looked none too pleased to find out that Daniel and I had other business to attend to for the afternoon.

I wasn't sure what "other business" was, but Daniel had insisted, using "the stateside board" as his excuse to take me away from my Afrikaans family.

"What? Ana Marie's brother getting saved?," I smiled at him. "It was a surprise to us, too, but he's totally into helping out with the DRC, and

Daniel, you wouldn't believe how great he is with the men out there. Sharing his faith, leading them to Christ, teaching them the Bible when I'm not even sure how he knows any of it himself yet –"

Daniel turned to face me. "Well, that's all great, but I guess what I'm more concerned about is... well, he was... a little into you."

"A little into me?," I asked. "Oh, he's harmless. Sure, he was a little aggressive at the beginning, before he became a believer –"

"Really now –"

"*But*, he's just fine now." I smiled. "He's just fine. Not a problem."

"It doesn't look like that to me," Daniel managed. "He seems a little too interested. Kissing you like that, buying you things –"

"Super Cs? Really?"

Daniel frowned at me. "Well –"

"And the kissing?" I put my hands on his face, planting a kiss on each of his cheeks. "When in Rome, Daniel. That's just what those old Afrikaner men do, and –"

"Oh, he's definitely not old enough for that –"

"Shame, man."

He frowned at me. "You know as well as I do that –"

"I *do* know as well as you do, which is why you should let me handle it." I smiled at him. "I'm a big girl, you know. I can take care of it. Been deflecting advances from enthusiastic men a whole lot longer than you have, Daniel."

He shook his head at me. "I'm a guy, and I know these things, and I know that old Vill-haaam –" I smiled at the exaggerated accent – "has other things on his mind when he looks at you."

"Shame, man," I said. "It's not like that."

He shrugged and blew out a breath. "I try to tell you, but you can't be told."

"Nope," I said, as I got in his truck. "So, what's this other business we have to take care of for the board?"

He shut the door behind me, then moved to his side to get in the driver's seat. "Oh, nothing." He smiled in my direction. "Just wanted to get you away from Super C back there."

"Duly noted," I smiled.


He informed me a few minutes later that in lieu of mission board business, we should spend the afternoon at the beach surfing, which was one of the only activities Swakop offered that he truly did enjoy. I found it incredible that Daniel would enjoy anything about my holiday town, but I kept my shock to a minimum as I informed him that I was an excellent swimmer and a fast learner.

And I was better than that. The coastline was horrific for surfing, but Daniel assured me that we would take what we could get. We had to swim far out to find any good waves at all, but once we did, I kept him properly impressed with my ability to do exactly as he did, with no previous experience at all. At several points, I did even better than he did, prompting those amazing, incredible smiles of his, as he laughed out loud in surprise.

"You've worn me completely out," he murmured at me, sitting up on his board, pulling mine closer to him, as I settled in.

"And it wore me out to do so," I smiled, adjusting my top for about the hundredth time that afternoon. His eyes drifted down to what I was doing, then snapped back up onto my face.

"You need to get a wetsuit," he said very simply.

"So, I won't be indecent, hmm?," I said softly, reaching up to retie my hair, considering only after I had done so that moving that way wasn't helping Daniel out much. "Maybe we should head back, huh? So I can get dressed?"

"Yeah," he managed, looking away from me. "Good idea."

Once we got back to the shore, grabbed our clothes out of his truck, and were sitting back on the seawall, dressed and covered in sand, I chanced a smile over at him.

"This was a good… break," I said.

"A break?," he said, smiling over at me. "This is hard, hard work, Sara."

"How so?," I asked, looking out at the water.

"Have to leave my thrilling life in Windhoek to come out here and check on the rogue missionary in the holiday town," he sighed.

"Rogue missionary," I smiled. "I love that."

"Yeah, the rogue missionary," he smiled back, "with her bizarre plans for a center."

"The center," I said, poking him in the shoulder, "that's working. So totally working."

"Mmmhmm," he nodded. "The Lord is still doing miracles, even today."

"You're so rude," I laughed at him.

"But that's not the worst of it," he said, laughing with me.

"Shame, man, you've been even ruder before," I said, "I remember."

"Shame, man," he said, imitating my voice.

"Yes, exactly. Proving my point," I replied, pulling my knees close and hugging them, leaning my head down and watching him coyly.

He watched me for a second, then looked out at the water again. "No, I meant that the bizarre ideas aren't the worst of what makes this particular girl," he grinned, "a rogue missionary."

"I'm a grown woman, Daniel, not a girl," I offered.

"Oh, I'm very, very aware of that," he said softly.

"What is it, then?," I managed. "What makes a rogue missionary?"

"Well, an addiction to Super Cs, the ability to seduce any and all Afrikaner men, and the inclination to walk the beach in a tiny little bikini."

"Shame, man," I gasped. "That *is* a rogue missionary!"

"Making my job hard, Sara," he said, giving me a stern look... then smiling.

"I shall have to watch myself," I said softly.

"You're starting to talk just like them," he said. "Do you hear yourself?"

"I don't talk to anyone else," I said simply. "This is what happens when they're the only people you have."

Daniel looked at me for a long moment. "You have me, too, Sara."

And we didn't say anything for a long while, until I broke his gaze, looking out at the water, resolving many things in my heart, then chancing a look back at him. He was still watching me.

"Sunset time," I murmured, my eyes intent on his. "Swakopmund's finest, you know."

"Mmm," he smiled, his hand covering mine on the seawall, never even glancing at the ocean.

"Daniel, you have to dance, too!"

Ana Marie grabbed him up from his seat, eliciting one of his incredible smiles. They were coming out more and more often by the minute, as I was seeing more of the same Daniel that had occupied my thoughts since we'd been up north. Still serious, still intense... but alluring and intoxicating and...

"Come on, Riaan," I shouted over the music in the little corner club we frequented often, prying my eyes off Daniel and trying to clear my head, "let's show them how it's done!" We had joined back up with Willem and the Bothas for dinner and dancing, and while Daniel had initially scowled at the prospect, given how tired we both were and how hesitant we both seemed to leave one another, even for the moment it would take to get cleaned up, he had agreed to come and had loosened up considerably over the evening. My friends just brought this lightness out in everyone.

"Have you stolen my partner?," Ana Marie grinned at me, as I linked my arm through her husband's. "He's not even that great of a dancer!"

"Oh, yes, he is. And besides, even if he was awful, he still has to be better than Daniel," I said, grinning and putting my hand to my mouth dramatically, pointing at him with my other hand, challenging him to get up and show us what he could do. "You should have seen him up north in the—"

"Hey, now," Daniel interrupted me.

"I'm not getting in the middle of this," Riaan laughed, letting go of my hand and grabbing Ana Marie up into his arms, twirling her away from us as she laughed with him.

Willem stood up. "Sara, let's show Daniel –"

"I've got it," Daniel muttered, pulling me to the dance floor and close to himself. "Now you've done it," he whispered in my ear.

"Done what?," I asked, breathless from being so suddenly close to him, keeping my head down lest he see the blush that was quickly spreading over my face.

"Now we have to watch Riaan and Ana Marie make out," he said.

Sure enough, that's exactly what they were doing, right there in front of everyone else on the dance floor, just as they had been doing most of the day around us.

"Shame, man," I said, wrapping my arms around him as we danced, turning my eyes away from the Bothas. "I'm not watching. That fixes that problem."

"Yeah," he whispered, "and then you've got Super C over there, practically salivating over you every time you –"

My eyes went to Willem, who was looking decidedly put out over being the only man without a partner. That wouldn't last long likely, though, with all the women casting glances his way.

"Daniel, he is *not* –"

"Sara, I'm not blind. And like I said, I'm not deaf, and me and ol' Boer Willem have had some words. Man to man words."

"I wondered about that. Shame, I wish I could understand you two. What were you talking about?," I smiled at him.

"About you, of course." He held my hand against his chest, smiling at me.

"Hmm... I'll bet that was a great conversation."

Daniel smiled. "Well, I can't translate all of it for you, obviously, because there aren't words for all of the Afrikaans phrases in English.

And if you think Willem is interesting in English, you should hear him in Afrikaans. His language is... colorful, to say the least."

"Shame, man," I laughed.

"Or maybe it's just me that brings that out in him," he laughed with me.

"Maybe if the two of you just went and had a good knockdown, drag out, you know? Maybe you'd get all of this out of your systems, buy one another a beer, and be BFFs afterwards."

He thought about this while glancing over at Willem. "Um... probably not."

"So," I said, taking a deep breath, "did you stand up for my virtue? Tell him to denounce all of his evil, scheming attempts to get in my pants –"

"Oh, geez, Sara –"

"Well, did you?"

He sighed. "No denouncing. We just settled on which one of us saw you first."

I felt my pulse flutter at this. "Well, I know who saw me first."

"Yeah?," Daniel asked, pulling me closer.

I smiled. "But I didn't think you were...well..."

"I am."

"Then," I murmured, "I know how to make this crystal clear for *both* of you, in any language." And without over thinking it, I put my hands in his hair, pulled his face down to mine, and kissed his lips softly and sincerely.

We watched one another for a long moment while everything around us seemed to freeze in place. I looked at him, my smile unsure, and whispered, "I should... should probably feel sorry that I did that, huh?"

He shook his head, a small smile still there, as he said, "Don't be... I'm not."

Our night concluded approximately two minutes later when Ana Marie, who was attempting to dip Riaan back in her arms, as the entire club cheered them on, dropped him flat on his back, tripped over him, and twisted her ankle. I was thankful for the brief respite from Daniel's penetrating gaze, even if it meant also giving up the security of being held in his arms on the dance floor.

"Shame, man!," Ana Marie yelled, as she and Riaan dropped me off at home. "This ruins *all* of our plans for tomorrow! I so wanted to finally take you to the dunes, Sara! And I don't want you to have to go by yourself," she said to me, pouting as though she was a small child being denied an ice cream cone.

"I'll take her," Daniel said, cutting off Willem before he could say it. "I don't have to be back until late tomorrow anyway."

"Good," Riaan smiled at him. "Will you come back soon so we can see you again?"

Daniel seemed to consider it. "Um... well, maybe. I have some trips down south to make soon, but maybe in another few weeks or so I'll come back through town."

"That will be just perfect!," Ana Marie squealed. "We will have the first batch of jewelry done by then. Right, Sara?"

"I hope," I said, holding up my crossed fingers.

"Stay with us next time," Ana Marie said to Daniel. "We have a guest room, and we can have a weekend long party at the Botha house. All of us! Or we can go camping! A braai! Lovey," she said to Riaan, "wouldn't that be great?"

Even in pain over her ankle, she was still inexhaustible.

"Sounds good," Daniel said, saying his goodbyes to all of us for the night, as Ana Marie winked at me, then drove away with Riaan.

I plopped on the sand dune next to him, exhausted. Daniel had scaled the same dune ten times in the time it took me to climb it once, and that was with all the breaks he took to sit at the top and laugh at me, as I discovered that you were either moving up or moving down – there was no staying still on this mountain of sand.

"I'm exhausted," I managed, as I brushed the sand off my hands. "And why didn't you tell me to wear flip flops?"

He grinned at me. "With the way you were climbing, you would have lost them and buried them completely before you even realized they were missing."

"Yeah, but now," I said, grabbing my ankles, "my sneakers are full of sand, and my socks, and – yeesh. It feels so grimy."

"Here," he said, pulling my feet into his lap, the simple movement making my head swim as he smiled at me. "Let's empty them out before we head down one last time."

I sighed as I leaned back, allowing him to unlace my shoes, looking over to the ocean, right as it met the dunes. Daniel had told me that it was one of the best contrasts in the whole country – this spot exactly, where the desert met the sea – the abrasive, hard, constantly shifting sand being thrust right up to the calm, soothing water, smoothing over its edges.

"I think I'm going to bring my parents here," I told him. "When they come and visit me next year."

"Already have visitors on your schedule," Daniel said, gently taking off my right shoe, a pool of sand falling all over his shorts as he did so. "Aren't you popular?"

"Popular with them," I smiled at him. "Only child and all. It's hard *not* to be popular when you've spent your entire life being only the lonely."

He nodded. "I'm an only child, too."

"No kidding," I laughed at him. "I couldn't tell, what with the way you always have to be in charge and how you have zero social skills."

"Hey," he laughed, holding onto my feet. "You better watch what you say to the man who can pull you up – literally – by your ankles."

"Okay, okay," I said, as he worked on taking off my other shoe. "You ever wish you had brothers and sisters?"

"No way," he said, glancing over my direction. "You?"

"Maybe a little. I have two friends who've always been like sisters, so maybe I had the best of both, you know?"

He nodded. "I'm glad it was just me. Things weren't good at home."

He didn't say anything for a long moment. Then, unexpectedly, "Where are you from, Sara?"

"Texas," I said. "Fort Worth."

"Texas," he said, emptying the sand out of the second shoe. "I knew there was some deeper reason behind the animosity you've always felt for me."

"Me? Well, there's animosity, but it hasn't been from me," I smiled at him. Again. "What's wrong with Texas?"

"Nothing, but Oklahoma always comes out on top, you know."

I couldn't help but laugh at him. "What?"

"Oklahoma, you know, that state on top of Texas," he said, laughing at me. "Do you want me to break out into song? Ooooooooohhhhh – kla-home-uh, where the –"

"Spare me," I said. "Are you from Oklahoma?"

"Yes," he said, beginning to work on my sand-filled socks. "A little town called Duncan, which I'm sure you've never heard of."

"Sure haven't," I said. "Your parents still live there?"

He shook his head. "Well, my mother does. I don't know my father." Then, pausing, staring at my toes and the nail art there. "How did you do that?"

"Ana Marie did that," I said. "It took her two hours to do that because she spent so much time talking. She was a little loopy after breathing all the fumes from the polish. Well, loopier than normal."

"That's fairly incredible," he managed. "Like miniature paintings."

I burst out laughing again, causing him to turn to me, self-consciously. "What?"

"It's just you," I said. "I never imagined when I met you that we'd be here, with you telling me that my toes look like works of art."

"I wouldn't have either. Mainly because I didn't know women even did this to themselves."

I leaned back on my elbows as he started in on the second sock. "I'm sure your mother had at least one pedicure in all of her life, Daniel. You just weren't paying attention."

He looked at me thoughtfully. "You don't know my mother," he said, his attention now on my second foot. "How does that feel? Less grimy?"

"Much better," I said, wiggling my toes as he brushed off the last of the sand. I tried to move my feet from his lap but stopped when I saw the intensity on his face.

"I'm not great at keeping in touch with home," he began. "I haven't been back in… years, actually."

"Really?," I asked. "No furlough?"

"None," he said. "And I don't hear much from my mother. It's been probably… three months or so since I've heard anything." He looked up at me. "She's sick. Congestive heart failure, I think was what she said."

"Daniel, I'm so sorry," I said.

"Well," he said, taking a breath and rubbing my foot distractedly. "It's just one of those things. She's never taken very good care of herself." He looked over at me. "The last time I saw her, she was… well, not good. Seminary graduation, which she managed to show up for. But that was because she needed to ask for money."

"Money?," I asked. "Is she… in financial trouble?"

He nodded. "Yeah… her own doing, of course." He looked over at me. "She has addiction problems. She's always had addiction problems. Heroin, meth."

I wasn't sure what to say to this. Daniel must have taken my silence for disbelief, as he added, "And I know what you're thinking. How in the world does an addict's son end up here, right?"

"It does seem out of the ordinary," I murmured, not knowing what part of Daniel's history I meant.

"Yeah," he said, looking out at the ocean. "Well, God is more faithful than people. Even if we don't deserve for Him to be."

"I'm sorry, Daniel."

"Sorry?," he looked at me, an uncertain smile on his face. "Why?"

"For... for all of that. I can't even imagine."

He nodded. "I'm glad that you can't. Really."

I leaned my head on his shoulder as he linked his fingers through mine.

"Hey, Sara," he said softly. "Is this...us... okay with you?"

I looked up at him. "Yeah," I said softly. "It is."

"Okay," he murmured, reaching down to touch my face and kiss my lips, just as the sun dropped down into the ocean and another day ended in Namibia.


To: Sara Wright (sarawright@gonowmissions.org)

From: Daniel Boyd (danielboyd@gonowmissions.org)

Subject: Expense reports

Sara, the board is requesting quarterly expense reports for the center. I've tried to tell them that you've curtailed pretty much all of the expenses for the center with donations from the US, but they don't seem to be able to believe it. Which is not surprising. Please send me something to send to them, even if it's just confirmation of what I've already explained to them.

And thanks for this weekend. I had a good time. I'll come back and see you soon.

Daniel

# 7 CHAPTER SEVEN

We were elbow deep in our projects when Daniel showed up, unannounced from Windhoek.

The ladies from the Dutch Reformed Church had come that day to do tea and share a Bible study from Matthew with the forty ladies who had been coming faithfully all along. Soon, we would have enough jewelry to ship a good portion to the States, where Grace Community Church, Iglesia Redeemer, and three other churches back in Texas were paying for them outright. I looked forward to being able to give the Namibian ladies their earnings, which far exceeded what we had predicted and which would feed their families for the next few months, as we made more stock for other churches already on our order list.

Daniel and I had been corresponding about the details, in our concise, clipped way. And we'd also been corresponding about things that had nothing to do with the work over phone calls that were long and lingering. In all the wonderful words shared across the kilometers, however, he had neglected to mention that he would be coming to the coast. At least, he neglected to mention it to me, but upon seeing him enter the building, Ana Marie leapt up from the place where she was helping with the paint to splay her arms out dramatically, shooting me a knowing smile and shouting, *"Surprise, Sara!"*

Daniel looked at her oddly, almost embarrassed, as I laughed.

"Hey," I said to him, taking off my glasses and putting down the work I was doing, as he walked in the door. "I didn't know you were on holiday." I smiled at this, the constant implication he made that I was always "on holiday" in my lovely seaside town.

"I knew he was coming," Ana Marie clapped her hands. "He's staying with me and Riaan and Willem. And then, he's going down to Luderitz with Willem later on in the week, right? Still? Should just be a day trip with the flight and all."

This was news. Great news. I had noticed more and more changes in Willem lately and could not have credited this to Daniel, who must have been speaking with him and making plans for ministry with him.

It was brilliant, actually, and perfect for Willem.

"Well, yes, actually," Daniel said, humoring me with a small smile. "Hoe gaan dit?," he greeted the ladies gathered there. They smiled up at him, smiled at me, and began making conversation amongst themselves, giggling as they did so. Ana Marie settled back down with them.

"I don't think they know that you understand," I whispered to him.

"Those ladies are speaking Damara," he said. "So they're right. I don't understand. Mr. Shiftoka understands Damara, though, which —"

"Which is why you wanted him here instead of me, I know, I know," I sighed, laying out a few of the necklaces we'd just completed.

He nudged my shoulder with his as he laid out another few necklaces beside mine, making a smile come to my lips unbidden. "Surely I never said that. Because that? Would have been stupid."

"Well," I said, "you did. And you were."

"Mr. Shiftoka couldn't have done all of this," he said, indicating the small makeshift warehouse we had set up. "It appears that God knew what He was doing after all."

I smiled at him. "I'll take that heavily-veiled compliment. Thank you."

He shrugged. Then, after a moment of silence. "Let me take you to dinner tonight." His eyes never left the table.

I reached over, straightening the necklace that he was laying out, my hand brushing his. "Okay."


Daniel was aggressive, much more so than I had occasionally dreamt he might be.

But he was nothing compared to me.

Dinner had been a very charged affair. Every look across the table, every touch – accidental and intentional – had produced another spark, another jolt of electricity, within both of us, it seemed, as we exchanged heated looks. Halfway through the entrées, my hand was on his knee underneath the table. Before our desserts even arrived, his hand was on my thigh. So by the time the check came, we were both pretty worked up. We had wandered out of the restaurant without a plan or a direction, holding hands, touching one another, and I allowed Daniel to tug me along with him as we headed towards the beach. Before long, we found ourselves in a dark corner of the Strand, where months of pent up frustration and attraction on my part exploded into need and desire when Daniel pulled me close and kissed me. It had been so long since I had been kissed like this, even longer since I had been held or even so innocently embraced, and even as my mind screamed at me to keep my distance, I couldn't help but pull him closer and encourage the advances he was hardly making. The fact that it was Daniel just sent me farther over the edge, as my mind mentally replayed all the many images of him that I had been treasuring in my heart all this time – him sitting on the seawall with his sunglasses on that first angry morning, lying on the side of the dunes and laughing as I struggled to make my way to the top, sharing the Gospel in a village up north, dancing much too close to me at a shebeen in Oshakati, taking off all of his clothes as he sauntered over to the Kunene River...

Yeah, that last one was making my kisses a bit more intense.

He seemed shocked at first, then only slightly hesitant, and finally, completely and wholly as wrapped up in needing me the way that I was needing him. With every touch, every inch of his body that my fingertips traced through his shirt, I felt my heart race faster and faster, until I could hardly think. He seemed to be having the same problem, as his own hands clenched the bottom of my shirt tightly, pulling it away from my shorts, his fingers finally gloriously touching the bare skin at my waist. I felt my breath catch in my throat as he caressed my back and his lips made their way down my neck. I knew exactly what I wanted.

"Come home with me," I whispered to him, knowing as I said it that it was wrong and yet repeating myself. "Come home with me now."

"Sara," he breathed, "I can't —"

"Please, Daniel," I insisted, pulling him even closer.

He didn't even waste time speaking, taking my hand in his rough way and all but dragging me back to his truck, where I slid in as close to him as I could get, putting my hand on his thigh, which made him drive even faster.

As he sped towards my flat, I turned towards him and began kissing his neck, my hands in his hair.

"Oh, wow, am I glad Mr. Shiftoka never made it across the Atlantic," he groaned appreciatively as he drove.

"I think I want you even more than I hated you at first," I managed in between kisses. "Are we almost there?"

"Well, I'm about to just pull off the road, and do–"

And then, he did. Before I could protest, I saw that he wasn't even looking at me anymore. I followed his gaze to—

"Oh, no! The center!"

Without thinking of safety, I jumped out of Daniel's truck and began running to the small warehouse we had been renting. The door had been all but destroyed in someone's anxious quest to get inside, and the entryway was unguarded and open.

"Sara, wait!" Daniel was two steps behind me, and just as I stepped over the threshold, his arms were around my waist, pulling me back. "Sara, they could still be in there!"

"I don't care," I said, my tears blinding me. "I have to see… to see what they've done!"

"You're not going to get yourself killed," he said, turning me around to face him. "Let me check it out."

"And get yourself killed?" I shook my head at his illogic. "I'm going in, too."

So, together, we went in, threw on the lights, and saw… saw it all. Destroyed.

I stood in stunned silence for a moment, looking at all those months of work, thrown all over the floor. And the money, the money I had already converted into Namibian dollars, and locked up in the lock box and stored away in a safe place –

"Oh, please, God, no," I ran over to where it was hidden, only to discover that it was gone.

All of it. Gone.

Daniel knelt down beside me, picking up a couple of broken necklaces as he did so, beads flying everywhere.

"Sara, I'm so sorry," he said softly.

I tried to swallow past the lump in my throat. It did nothing to stop the tears from spilling over my cheeks.

"It... it just happens sometimes," Daniel said, putting his hand on my shoulder.

"This happens?" I looked at him, wiping away tears with back of my hand. "Everything gets destroyed? It *happens*?"

"It wasn't your fault," he said.

"No, it's just my own stupidity," I said. "I should never have left the money here. And that door? I should have done something. A better lock or something, like you told me. I just... I should've known better. Haven't you been warning me all this time, since the first day I got here?"

"But, Sara, you have to look at —"

"No! You were right! It just... it can't be helped. And this is the kind of thing that happens when people try to help other people. And I was a fool for thinking that this would work out."

"No," he said, heated, turning me to look him in the eyes. "I was *wrong*. This was a good thing, a very good thing, and it still can be, if—"

"The money is *gone*! How am I going to replace that? How am I going to feed these women now? And after they've supported themselves for two weeks... then what? We'll just start over again, so this can happen a hundred more times?"

"We can figure it out, just —"

"I hate this place!," I yelled. "I hate everything about it!"

Daniel sat silently for a moment. Then, quietly, "We can get this taken care of. You have to trust me."

"What gets me the most is that you tried to tell me this! And you tried to warn me. And goodness knows, everything about *your* ministry was going great without me coming here and making these women dependent on money that I've now lost. What kind of hope have I even given them? Did I even make any difference at all for Christ?"

"Look at the Bothas. And Willem. You've done so much here. And I think if you just −"

I couldn't stop the tears from falling. "Yeah, let's talk about what I've done, Daniel. I mean, tonight, right? Just a little while ago. With you."

He backed away from me, fractionally, and took a breath. "What does that mean?"

"It means," I said, "that I'm doing more damage than good most of the time, right? Losing all of this money, putting these women in a *worse* situation, and... doing all that I can to destroy your ministry and witness simply because I'm so unbelievably, pathetically *needy*. Here I am, wanting you, seducing you, and begging you to take me to bed, just because I'm so lonely that I feel like I could die here without anyone ever noticing that I'm... that I'm missing at all."

Finally, I had said something that made him silent. "Is that what... is that what it was all about?"

"What? What part of all that stood out to you?"

"The part about... wanting me. Was it just about being lonely?"

This made me cry harder. "Is that all you heard, Daniel? Here I am, pouring out my heart about everything, and all you heard was the part about *you*? How is everything done here, no matter what, all about *you*? I'm here, too! I'm part of this team, too!"

A look of anguish crossed his face, as he started to speak again, "No, Sara, I didn't mean it like that. It's just—"

"I should *never* have come here!," I shouted at him, hating the hurt there in his eyes. I had been foolish to believe that I could make any difference here, when all I felt all the time was so needy, so deficient, so unable to do anything but wreak havoc with my actions. "Daniel, when I think of what happened tonight here – all of the loss experienced here – I just feel sick. And then when I think of what *could* have happened, with you and me, what I still *want* to happen, even now as I know it shouldn't, and how it would destroy your ministry if the board found out – I feel completely worthless. Why am I even here? What good am I doing?"

"You're not the only one culpable for these things, Sara," he said. "We can fix this," he indicated the mess around him, "and it will get better." He looked at me for a moment, a familiar hardness coming to his face. "And as for us... well, if that's really how you feel, then –"

"Daniel, that's not what I meant. I –"

"No, it's done. Fine. I get it."

We stood staring at one another for a moment. He wasn't hearing me. He had stopped listening. And all the trust we had built up between one another? Was just gone. Just like that. Finally, I spoke.

"I just want to go home. Alone. Please take me home."


Someone was banging on my door much too early for a Saturday morning.

My face was wrecked from all the tears I had cried the night before, and my head was throbbing from the drama of all that had happened. I hadn't even bothered to change my clothes or turn off the lights when Daniel had left me alone, and seeing everything the same as it had been, yet so drastically different now in the light of day, left me feeling worse about the whole situation.

What had I been thinking? Well, I actually knew exactly what I had been thinking down at the Strand, my hands all over Daniel, my mind running over the past months and all that he had come to mean to me. But why had I had such trouble censoring my thoughts, my actions, and inevitably my words as I spoke so harshly to him? Why had I not shown any reservations in sending him away so coldly when all I really wanted inside was to drag him back up the stairs with me and never let him leave my flat?

And then, the center. All the money gone, all the product wasted. All those months of hard work and all those women depending on me. Would I be a coward if I just left now and never, ever looked back?

"Sara! Get up already!" I could hear Ana Marie moving away from the front door, mercifully ceasing her banging on it… then beginning to bang on my bedroom window. "I know you're in there! Daniel said to come and get you!"

"Daniel?," I asked out loud, stumbling over to the front door, opening it to her excited face. "You've been talking to Daniel?"

"Ja! We were a bit worried when he never showed up last night, and Riaan had half a mind to come over here and drag him out of your room. With his knickers around his ankles, too, I'd imagine."

My face blazed red hot at the implication… and the very near truth of it.

"Ana Marie," I gasped. "We *never* –"

"Sara, I know that. But we're looking out for you now, and with the way the two of you look at one another, well it's easy to see that–"

"He wasn't here," I said softly.

"Shame, man, I *know* he wasn't here," she smiled at me, "because he showed up early this morning and told us what he'd been doing all night. The center, the break in, *all* of it, and he had been working to fix what had been destroyed. He even got Willem to come down there and help him."

"He did?"

"Ja, and you need to come with me now so we can see what's what with the center," she said, dragging me out to the car, where Riaan waited behind the wheel.

It was true. Daniel had been working all night, and somehow, he had salvaged half of the work. Willem had also helped him to fix the door and the two of them were, at this very moment, in town arranging for a security system and a better lock, according to Riaan.

At least this calamity had bonded the two of them. That could only mean good news for the future of the center. And for the future of the ministry they were planning in other parts of the country.

"Daniel was determined to make it right for you, Sara," Riaan said to me. "And he showed us what needed to be fixed, and we've talked with the ladies. They should be here this afternoon, and we're going to get it all done. Plenty of time left before we need to post it all anyway, you know."

"But the money –" I began.

"It's actually all taken care of," Daniel said, from where he now stood just outside the door, his back turned to me as he inspected what he and Willem had already fixed. "There was room in the mission's budget this quarter. We'll have to change some of our plans for outreach in the north, but your ladies will be taken care of. And they'll still have incentive to keep working on the next batch, so that the center can continue on."

I knew what this cost him. And somehow, around the lump in my throat, I managed a weak, "Thank you, Daniel."

He never even turned around to look at me.

After Ana Marie and Riaan had gotten the ladies started on what we would need to finish for the day, I borrowed their car and made my way to their house, where Daniel was catching up on the sleep he'd lost the night before, thanks to me. I used their key to get inside, where I waited in the kitchen and could hear the shower running.

I had to apologize. I had to make things right. I had to fix this today so that I could keep working here.

Though it was more than that.

I was so embarrassed by my behavior the night before – all of it – and at the potential it had to ruin what had been a good working relationship and make it into a series of awkward, humiliating interactions for the rest of my term here. And beyond it being a working relationship... well, I cared for Daniel more than I had planned on caring for him certainly, but as time went by, I began to feel myself hopelessly feeling more than was definitely wise, especially given the insane nature of the man who these feelings were directed towards and –

"Geez, Sara!," I heard from over my shoulder. "Could you try knocking on the door next time?"

I couldn't see him anywhere. "Where did you go?"

"I'm trying to get to my clothes," he said. "They're in the guest room."

Of course, to get to the guest room from the bathroom, he'd have to walk through the kitchen. Crazy Namibian house.

"Sorry, sorry," I muttered, blushing and rushing to the living room.

"Okay, it's all clear. And I'm... well, I'm not looking."

I could hear him walk through, exasperated, then slam the door behind him. Ten seconds later, it was open again.

"Well? Why are you here? Is something wrong at the center?"

I peeked over my shoulder, relieved to see that he was wearing shorts at least, alarmed to see that he still hadn't put on a shirt. As if I needed any more distractions or temptations today.

"Nothing's wrong at the center," I managed. "It's all great, actually, thanks to you, Riaan, Willem, and Ana Marie. And all the ladies, of course."

"Hmm," he managed.

And then, I saw it. The bruise on his face, the beginning of a black eye.

"Oh, my word, Daniel, what happened? Did the guy who broke into the center come back and... hit you?"

"What?," he asked, then with some realization. "Oh, no. This?" He indicated his face. "Compliments of Willem."

I gasped. "Shame, man."

"Oh, he looks just as bad. Well, maybe not quite as bad. He's one big, burly guy."

I was astounded. "Why were you two fighting?"

"Well," he snapped at me. "Seems ol' Willem saw us on the Strand, you know, with your hands all over me. But from *his* vantage point, it was *my* hands that were all over *you*, and he found me after I left your place. Told me a thing or two about respecting a woman – which is really ironic and all, considering his own sordid past, the details of which he shared with me after we finally beat the crap out of one another and were having a heart to heart chat."

"Oh, no," I whispered.

"Oh, it's all good now," Daniel muttered sarcastically. "Once we got our breath back and declared it an even fight, we had a couple of beers together and are now on our way to being BFFs, just like you said we would. Hooray for that, right?"

"Daniel –"

"Got any other huge Afrikaans men protecting your virtue, Sara? Because I'd like to explain last night to them before they break any more blood vessels in my freakin' face."

"No, I'm so sorry... oh, Daniel. I'm sorry."

He shrugged. "It's fine. He was a big help afterwards, getting everything cleaned up. And he even wanted to talk about some plans for ministry in the parts of the country he tours. Then, he spent two more hours sharing the Gospel with me so emphatically and so convincingly as we worked on all that tiny jewelry together that I was ready to get saved all over again! So... maybe us beating one another to a bloody pulp was all for the best." He sighed. "And you have no idea how bizarre that is."

"It wasn't all for the best," I managed. "Last night... I'm sorry."

He said nothing for a moment. "Sorry... for what?"

"For all the things I said, okay? For getting upset and biting your head off. And for coming onto you and practically attacking you on the Strand. Not my finest moment, you know."

"You see," he said, rubbing his chin, "that's not how I remember it."

"Oh?"

"No, it seems that I came onto *you*, according to Willem. And after thinking about it this morning, more than I probably should? I tend to agree with him. I was taking advantage of a situation. Clearly."

This took me aback. "You don't seem like the kind of guy who takes… well, takes advantage. Especially with… well, with all that's been happening between us, and –"

"You don't know me all that well, though, do you?"

This was true. I didn't. "You're not like that, though. You meant what you did. You weren't taking advantage of me when I was just as into it as you were."

He looked at me with an antagonistic expression on his face. "Really?" He walked slowly over to me, until we were standing inches apart from one another. "What would you say if I told you that the Bothas are, I'm assuming, unable to get back in this house since you likely have their car *and* their keys—"

"I do," I managed in a shaky voice.

"—leaving us completely alone together for the entirety of the afternoon? And what would you say if I told you that I've spent every night for the last month, ever since we came back from the north, dreaming of you, wanting to touch you, imagining any number of scenarios that would involve me finally having you when I want you, without anyone knowing or any consequences at all? Would you trust me then? Do you trust me now?"

I could feel my face blazing as my head and my heart screamed frenzied affirmations. But I kept my hands to my sides and, mustering up all the self-control I had, began to tell him that I –

Fortunately, the front door opened before I could betray myself. And as we heard loud footsteps echo through the hall, I blew out the breath I'd been holding in and took a step back from Daniel, just as Willem stepped into the kitchen. "Sara, lovey! Hoe gaan dit?," he offered looking from one of us to the other.

"Baie, baie goed, Willem," I said, still a bit breathless as Daniel continued staring at me. "I do appreciate all your help with… well, the center. And everything else you did last night."

He grinned at me wickedly, glancing over at Daniel. "Oh, it was my pleasure."

"Hey," Daniel said towards him, finally taking his eyes off of me. "You look like crap, man."

Willem smiled at him. "I feel like… crrrrrrap." His accent was horrible. "Is that the English word for…"

"Sure is," Daniel affirmed.

"Ahh, will add it to my list of words," he laughed. He did, in fact, look like crap. Daniel obviously hadn't been the biggest dog in the fight but there was still a lot of fight in him. Willem was sporting just as many bruises and even had fingernail scratches on his neck.

"Oh, geez," I murmured, looking at him, then glancing back at Daniel, who managed a shrug.

"Doesn't hurt a bit," Willem said. "I've had much worse. Sorry to… interrupt things. But I haven't showered in quite a while, and with all the work last night –"

"Go ahead," Daniel said. "I didn't leave you a drop of hot water."

"Dankie, friend," Willem laughed. "Hot water is for sissies anyway."

And he left the room, leaving me alone with Daniel again. Bolstered by the confidence that came with having some accountability in the very next room, I tried to apologize again.

"I'm sorry."

He shook his head, sitting down at the kitchen table and leaning back to look at me. "Well, I appreciate that. But it doesn't make things better.

This is a recurring theme with you lately. You bring out all of these things in me that I... well, that I hate actually."

"Such as?"

"Well, all of these things I thought I already knew with some certainty, you're blowing out of the water. Like this whole center thing? It doesn't make good sense, and it doesn't have *anything* to do with what we had planned for the rest of the country. But you came in, did it, took half of my budget to salvage it, and now? Well, now the board wants *you* to tell *me* how to do a job I've been doing here for ten years."

"Daniel, I —"

"Oh, the work is great. And you've gone above and beyond, likely, by meeting these people, winning them to Christ, and providing me with the *perfect* national missionary to the parts of the country I haven't even had time to get to. A pilot. An Afrikaner pilot who, God help us all, has a burden to preach the Gospel. How did you do that? How did you do, in mere months, what I haven't been able to do in ten years?"

I fought the tears that were threatening to fall from my eyes. "It wasn't me."

"But I hate how much being around you and being around all of this is showing me how I just don't have it all figured out and how I'm rude, stupid, arrogant, and pompous? Was that the word you used to describe me once?"

"Well, yeah. I probably did use that word. But —"

"And then!," he continued on. "Then, I open up to you because you're beautiful and incredible and amazing and you're looking at me like I'm some wonderful guy or something, and I tell you all of this stuff about my mother and my miserable childhood, and I think I'm actually falling in love with you, and when I get carried away by it all and try to *show* you what I'm feeling, you come back and tell me that the only reason you're looking at me that way is because you're so lonely."

I was stunned. "Daniel, I... " I caught myself before I could reveal too much, and went back to the only thing he had said that really mattered. "Daniel, are you falling in love with –"

He exhaled sharply. "I think I need to be done for a while, Sara. Can we agree to that? To stay out of one another's way for a while? And to revisit this whole thing and get back to a working relationship when I can get past feeling anything but complete derision and loathing for myself when I'm in your presence, okay?"

I felt myself choke up over so many opportunities and moments lost, over all the tenuous trust between us that had shattered and fallen to pieces like all of the jewelry that had sparked the whole thing.

Without another word, I rushed away from the Botha house and from him.


The phone call from the States came later that day from a board member who had no clue what was happening on the ground in Namibia. They had no idea what Daniel had salvaged, what it had cost him to save the day for me, and how alienated I had made him in my frustration. The missionary they sent to make a new way for women had done her very best to rip apart what was already effective on the field, all by ruining the only missionary who had made any kind of difference here at all.

They didn't know any of it.

"Sara, we're asking you to come back for a few weeks. Bryan and Christy Murphy are back stateside, and we want the three of you to make several presentations at some different state meetings. We want our trustees to hear about the amazing things that are happening with this center concept that you've all made succeed so well."

It would be good to see Bryan and Christy again, even if it felt as though my ministry was a complete sham. And the break from Namibia, and from Daniel, would do me good.

"I would be happy to. When should I be ready to leave?"

# 8 CHAPTER EIGHT

"And then what?," she said, taking yet another bite.

Emily was more into my story than I had thought she would be. I had been back in the US all of twelve hours when she and Melissa arrived at my parents' house, picked me up, and drove me back to Melissa and Beau's, where we had been eating and talking non-stop.

Well, we had all three been doing the talking, but most of the eating? Had been done by Emily.

"Do I need to call Josh and have him stage an intervention?," Mel asked, regarding the three bowls of chili Em had just finished. "Because I'm thinking the man who has to sleep with your pregnant self tonight needs to be aware that you've just consumed more chili in thirty minutes than I've eaten in the entire past year alone, and —"

"*It's all that sounds good!*," Emily growled at her. Then, a thoughtful moment later. "Well, this and honeybuns. Do you have any honeybuns?"

"*No,*" Mel yelled, then looked over at me. "Okay, so go on. We want to hear the rest of the story!"

I sighed, picking up where I had left in my story of the evening I'd spent with Daniel, right about the moment that we left half our food behind at the restaurant so as to put our hands and our mouths to better use. "Well, then, I... well, tried to get him into bed."

Emily began choking on her chili.

"Sounds like he was already heading that way," Mel pointed out. She leaned forward eagerly, ignoring our choking friend in the process. "And then what?"

"Em, are you okay?," I asked, concerned about the way her eyes were watering and she was gasping for breath.

"Oh, yeah," she wheezed. "Just went down the wrong way. But, please, keep talking. This is the most exciting story I've heard in... well, ever, actually."

"Well," I said, "he was all for it, I thought. Um, we jumped in the truck, started driving, and *that's* when we discovered the break-in."

"But he fixed it all," Emily said. "Right? Took care of everything, just like a real hero, right?"

"Yeah," I said. "And then he told me, basically, that he needed space. That I... make him feel worthless."

Mel sat back for a minute. "Is he crazy?"

I frowned at her. "No, he's not crazy."

"He has issues," Emily said, very simply. "And it breaks my heart to say it, because he sounds amazing."

I bit my lip. "Well, we all have issues."

"Yes, we do," Mel offered. "But your inclination to... well, to hitch yourself up to guys that have *big* issues is just —"

"What issues did Jon have?," I asked, irritated.

"Well, there was the infidelity," Emily began.

"The fear of commitment," Mel added.

"And the way he totally began to *obsess* over you once you moved overseas," Emily concluded. "Twenty calls in one weekend, and –"

"Okay," I admitted. "Those are issues. But Daniel –"

"Has even worse issues!," Mel exclaimed. "I know you like him, Sara, but... are you prepared for what comes with being with someone like him? Who, from what you tell us, is angry, melancholy, confusing, and gets worked up over –"

"I don't know," I said simply. "And there's something more there, that... well, that must explain it. That must explain why he feels like he does and acts like he does and... well, he's not all bad. Have I made him sound completely bad?"

"No," Emily sighed. "You make him sound like he's wonderful and incredible and... well, like you're completely in love with him. And you're making me fall for him, too."

"You're married," I said, narrowing my eyes at her, teasingly.

"Oh, I know," she said. "But Josh? Would take a plate of empanadas over a steamy evening with me, frankly."

"Must be all the chili," Melissa murmured quietly.

"I heard that," Em said, frowning. "And it's probably true, but whatever. I like chili."

I smiled. "Anyway, it's not like I have a choice right now, in being with him or not being with him, not with the way he's shut me out."

Mel and Em both looked at me with harsh expressions.

"What?," I asked.

"Please," Emily said. "You know he's probably trying to call you right this second, sorry for what he said."

"I don't think you know him," I said, hopeful that maybe this was the case.

"And I'm not sure that you do either," Melissa said softly. "As much as you need to probably."

This was a given. There were many unanswered questions and concerns and –

"Just be careful, okay?," Mel asked. "And maybe... figure out what's really going on. While you're here. Before you go back and face him again."

The presentations were, as Ana Marie would say, hectic.

Bryan, Christy, and I barely had time to reacquaint ourselves before being thrown headlong into a series of presentations for board members, stateside personnel, and trustees, all of whom were receptive enough to what we were saying, even though we had little to no time to adequately prepare for the message we shared, given the few days we had been granted for the task.

Before we were each sent back to our home cities to be flown to our destination countries again, Christy made sure that we had time to talk with one another.

"How's Africa?," she asked, smiling as we sat down for coffee, just a few hours before we were set to leave for our flights.

As I sipped my drink, I thought about the mess I had left behind. "Just great," I said softly.

"Really?," she said, tilting her head to the side and studying me for a second.

So, I told her the positives – Ana Marie and Riaan coming to faith, all their work, Willem doing likewise and shocking us all, the center, the work we had gotten done, the work that was up ahead –

"I can't believe you've managed to do so much all by yourself out there," she said. "We heard that there's only one other missionary in the country. And that he isn't even in the same town."

"No, he isn't," I said, very simply. "But I've gotten to know him... with all the administrative things that needed to be done for the center, of course."

"What does he think about it all? Does it fit into the strategy he already had in place for the ministry there?"

I thought about this and replied, "Um... kinda."

"And by that, you mean..."

"Not at all," I smiled at her. "But plans change, right?"

"They sure do," she sighed. "And for the better sometimes." She stayed silent for a moment. "You seem preoccupied, Sara."

"Me? Well, it's been a busy week."

"Tell me about it." She set her own drink down. "Okay, so what's *really* going on?"

I put my drink down as well, ready to tell her everything... then thought better of it. It was no one's business but mine and Daniel's, wasn't it? And even though I had told my friends about my feelings, about Daniel himself, I hadn't mentioned his mother, the cryptic allusions he'd made to his past, and all the suspicions I had about why Daniel was who he was. It hadn't been my information to share, and now? It still wasn't.

Still, though. Christy was connected. And I knew she could point me in the direction of the right answers.

"Actually," I began, choosing my words carefully, "I need to get in touch with... well, my teammate's mother while I'm stateside. And I haven't had a chance to yet, obviously, so it's been weighing pretty heavily on me."

"Is everything okay?"

"Well, she's sick," I said, giving her this much, "and I thought I could check on her for him, you know?"

"Of course," Christy said, nodding. "Do you have her contact information?"

"I sure don't," I sighed. "Do you think you could use one of your contacts at the board to find it out for me?"

"Absolutely," she smiled, pulling out her phone to call her contact. "What's his name?"

"Daniel Boyd," I said softly, wondering at the wisdom of any of this.


Finding Daniel's mother had not been easy, as she wasn't listed on his emergency contact information. The fact that no one was listed for Daniel was a bit of a shock to the personnel department of the board, who, as Christy sat on the phone with them, her eyes rounding periodically at the strangeness of a man with no family history or records, set to work on finding the information for their own files.

They were able to find a permanent address for him but had no idea if it was still current, communicating to me through Christy that I needed to communicate this to Daniel. Christy and I did some research of our own afterwards, finding the name of Daniel's mother, which wasn't easy since she had long since stopped going by the name Boyd. I couldn't figure out if it had been her maiden name or a married name or if it was even legitimately Daniel's, but she was now going by Miller. It took several calls back to the board to update them on this, a lot of research online, and a hunch or two, but I finally had an address in hand by the time I arrived back in Texas, where I quickly made a plan.

"Hey, Emily," I said, after she answered her phone.

"Hey, you're back!," she said. "Are we still on for lunch with Melissa today?"

"I'm going to have to cancel," I said. "I'm sorry, but... something's come up."

"Well, I'll miss seeing you again," she sighed. "But I understand."

"Actually, I'll still probably see you... when I come to borrow your car so that I can drive to Oklahoma," I said, crossing my fingers that she'd agree.

"Absolutely," she said. "Are you coming by right now?"

"Well, yeah... aren't you going to ask why I'm going there?"

A pause. "I'm assuming it has something to do with Daniel. And that it's none of my business. If you'll just tell me the name of the town, so at least one person knows where you are if something happens, I don't need to know any more."

"Thanks, Emily," I breathed. "I'm going to Duncan."


Three hours later, I was there.

Daniel's hometown was small but not without its own charm. I had driven through several nice neighborhoods and a bustling downtown before arriving in a more rundown, depressing neighborhood, and confirming against the address I had written down that this sad house, with peeling exterior paint and neglect evident in so many places, was where Daniel had grown up.

Taking a deep breath, I checked my alibi – an envelope with some money from my own account and a copy of the picture of Daniel from Ruacana Falls – and resolved again to simply tell her that he sent me to check on her while I was in town. It wasn't the truth, of course, but it was the only way I could explain my presence to her, to myself, as I wanted answers to why Daniel was the way he was.

I knocked on the door confidently, biting my lip as I waited for a response. It came half a minute later, as an older woman with Daniel's brooding eyes but none of his attractiveness opened the door.

"Yeah?," she asked, looking at me with no small amount of confusion.

"Hi," I began, surprised by the soft emotion in my voice. "Are you... Joanne Miller?"

"Yeah," she said. "Who are you?"

"Sara. Sara Wright. I work with your son. I work with Daniel."

She managed a small smile. Her face was older than her age, her color very bad, her illness showing itself with every labored breath. "Oh, well." Then confused, "How are you here then? Isn't Daniel still in... Africa somewhere?"

She didn't even know where in Africa. "Um... yeah. I'm just on assignment here in the States for a few days, and I... well, Daniel asked me to come by and check on you."

She gave me a disbelieving look. "Did he?"

I nodded, biting back any more lies. "And he asked me to give you this," I said, holding out the envelope to her.

She took it without her eyes leaving mine. "You wanna come in?"

"Yes, please," I said, following her into the dimly lit front room, where a television blared and something simmered on the stove in the kitchen.

"Let's see here," she said, opening up the envelope, nodding at the cash. "He's always good about sending money," she murmured. "He's a good man."

I thought on the truth of this. "He is. He's a wonderful man."

She glanced up at me, a knowing look in her eyes. Then, she pulled out the picture I had taken and sighed. "Well. He looks like his father. More and more, the older he gets." She smiled at me. "Which is a dirty shame, isn't it? That a man can look that good and be... well, you know Daniel."

And be belligerent? Stubborn? So angry, all the time? Yeah, I knew this. But I didn't know the why behind it.

"Is he... coming back anytime soon? Back to the US?," she asked softly.

I shook my head. "I don't think so."

She put the envelope down, propping the picture up against the lamp on the end table, lighting a cigarette for herself once her hands were free. "That figures. My son, missionary to Africa and all," she smiled, a doubtful look on her face.

"He's really good at what he does," I managed, not sure why I felt the need to defend Daniel to his mother like this.

"Oh, I'm sure he's good at *lots* of things," she smiled at me suggestively. "Especially with a pretty girl like you. What did you say you do in Africa?"

"I... well, Daniel and I work on the same team together. Visit people, share Christ with them, try our best to meet their needs."

"Hmm." She looked at me doubtfully.

I thought about my first day with Daniel. "Actually," I said. "Daniel does more than that. He shows up in a place, where children are dying from disease, and I swear to you, it's like Jesus in blue jeans has shown up with the way the people crowd around him, needing his help. And he speaks their language, understands their hurts, and he just... he just does what he can, and it's better than anyone else can do. Better than I can do certainly."

She exhaled a thin line of smoke. "My boy does that?"

I nodded. "It's incredible. Who he is. Who he... well, who he turned out to be. Considering and all."

I could imagine a younger Daniel here, dealing with this cynical woman, enduring her addictions and her problems, struggling to survive in this environment, much less flourish.

"Well, you seem to know him pretty well, then," she sighed. "Let me tell you something. I tried my best. Honest to God, I tried my best. But the state? Wouldn't let me even keep him here."

"Pardon?," I asked lamely, realizing that I had missed a huge chunk of Daniel's story.

"Yeah, I could've done better, but they were always taking him away," she shrugged. "And whatever, you know. Maybe they thought they could do better than I was doing. Dragging him out of here crying when he was so little, bringing back this sullen, angry boy in his place. And they thought it was better, you know." She pointed her finger at me. "But I can guarantee you that it wouldn't have gone down the way it did when they sent him to that group home if they'd just left me to take care of him."

"The group home," I said, having no idea what she was talking about, but desperately hoping that I would hear more, understand better, maybe solve the mystery behind Daniel. "Yeah, that."

"And it was all over the papers for *months*. Everyone *knew* what had happened," she said. "And my boy, practically a man, being forced to talk about what they'd done to him there, what they'd done to all of those little boys, and… Daniel was the one could end it all by talking about it. And he did. And what did they do? Sent him right back out to some other foster home without even a pat on the back. I could have done better, I tell you. Even at my *worst*, I could have done better."

And suddenly, I felt very sick, with a great majority of the pieces falling into place. Oh, Daniel…

"I wasn't the best mother to him," she started in again. "I had problems. But I could've done better than they did. He's a good son, though, even with all that happened. Even now, he sends money, makes sure I'm okay, you know."

I nodded, my need to be out of this house now urgent. "Well, I won't take up anymore of your time," I said to her, standing up. "Just wanted to drop that off for him and say hello to you."

She stood with me. "Send him my best," she said, walking me to the door, then closing it in my face without another word.

I didn't remember any of the drive back to Fort Worth. My mind was racing from the moment I left Daniel's childhood home… or at least the home he known every once in a while. All of these details about what he had endured, what he had suffered, and how it all contributed somehow to who he was now. Untrusting, defensive, and so angry.

Common sense would have told me to keep my distance. To let him be. To know when someone was beyond my help. To know when it would actually be futile and hopeless to put my emotions at risk in loving someone –

But I never listen to common sense on the small things. So, why would I listen to it when it came to Daniel and how much I loved him already?

Emily was waiting for me when I pulled up at her house. "Hey, how did it go?," she asked nervously.

"Worse than I thought. It's... not okay," I said, handing her the keys to her car.

"How bad is it?," she asked.

"It's a long story. And a mess. But Daniel?" I paused for a moment, not knowing how to put this to words.

"Yes?," Em asked softly.

"I love him," I said, very simply. "And that's enough."

"Oh, Sara," she sighed.

"I know," I groaned. "And after you warned me to protect my heart and all. Which I should have."

"But maybe you were supposed to be protecting your heart so that... so that you'd be ready for him," she said. Then, she began crying. "Oh, pregnancy hormones," she sobbed. "I'm just... concerned. And happy for you, all at the same time. Because I get that this? Is different than with Jon. And when you talk about Daniel, I get that he's someone very special. Even with whatever else is all wrapped up in this."

"He's going to be okay. And I will be, too. Can you keep praying for us?"

"Of course," she said, hugging me close. "Of course."

I got Christy's phone call the same day I arrived back in Walvis Bay. I was in the taxi that was to take me back to Swakopmund when her call came in on my cell phone.

"Sara!," she shouted. "I can't believe I got a hold of you!"

"Yes," I told her. "Just got in. This is the most expensive call ever, you know."

"I know, I know!," she said apologetically. "But I had to let you know that your teammate? Well, his mother passed on two days ago. Right after you left."

"Passed on?," I sat up straighter in my seat. "But she was…" I stopped myself from saying that she was fine when she had been anything but fine.

"Sara, you must have known more than you were letting on," Christy said. "That woman, she was a lifelong heroin user. She was fortunate to have lived as long as she did. Did you know? Did you know what you were getting into when you went to visit her?"

"I suspected," I murmured. "She wasn't well."

"Well," Christy sighed, "if anything good has come of it all, of what you did in tracking her down, it's that they knew about her, knew about her passing, and were able to tell your teammate. Geez, Sara, is he just a teammate? Because the secrecy would suggest that –"

"No, Christy, no," I breathed out, wondering if this had done any good at all, all that I had unearthed and started. "He's more than that."

She spoke softly, hurt by my omissions obviously but still strangely understanding. "Then you need to know that… well, the board got in touch with him to offer to fly him back to make arrangements, but he refused to leave. And now, they're concerned about him, and you're the only other personnel there. They want you to find him and make sure he's okay."

"They've never cared before," I said. "I mean, how long has he been out there without them even knowing his next of kin, and –"

"They care now," she said softly. "He's… he's got problems, Sara."

I knew this too well. And his number one problem at the moment? Was in a cab to Swakopmund via Walvis Bay. And I had started the whole terrible process of all of Daniel's past washing itself right into his life here in Namibia.

"It's all coming out now. All of it," Christy said.

"Okay, I'll get in touch with him."

Daniel was hard to track down.

I called the Windhoek office, only to have Emmanuel tell me that Daniel and Willem had been all over the country since I'd been gone. Down to Luderitz and Keetmanshoop a week ago, out to Swakopmund to check on the center, then up to the north, where the board had managed to track him down at the mission house in Tsumeb.

"Is he still there? In Tsumeb? Is Willem there?," I asked Emmanuel, as my taxi pulled into Swakopmund.

"No, Willem is back in Swakop. Just spoke with him on the phone earlier. As for Daniel and Tsumeb? Don't really know, Princess, but I can tell you where the extra key is at the house if you want to go there tonight to see."

I tapped the taxi driver on the shoulder. "Hey, do you want to make a whole lot of extra money? It's out of your way, but I'll make it worth it."

"Where to, miss?"

"Tsumeb, please."

# 9 CHAPTER NINE

Several hours later, we pulled into Tsumeb, just as the sun was setting. I paid the taxi driver generously for his trouble, then took my suitcases in my hands, and began walking the dirt road toward the mission house. How things had so changed since my last trip down this road with an uncharacteristically amused Daniel, pointing things out to me as we walked and discussed plans for what could be done here. I walked with my heart in my throat, thinking of all that had been said and all the many things that had still been left unsaid between us.

As I rounded the corner to the house, my eyes easily found Daniel in the last of the Namibian sun's setting rays, as he sat on the roof of the house, shirtless and hard at work, prying off shingles with his bare hands, his back to me.

He called out to me in Oshiwambo, hearing my noisy footsteps, and when I didn't respond, he turned to face me, tossing a shingle down as he did so.

"Ahh," he said, turning back to his work. "If it isn't Miss Wright, the board's ambassador to the masses. Nice vacation in the States, hmm?"

I took a breath, dropping my luggage right in the road. I could understand his irritation with me over my abrupt departure and all that we had left unresolved. "Daniel, I heard about your mother."

"Yes, dear old Mom," he said, tossing down the last shingle, glancing at me. "Did they tell you that she had blown through every last cent I ever sent her so that there was nothing left for burial costs?"

I shook my head.

"Watch out," he warned, before jumping straight off the roof.

"Daniel, that's dangerous," I said, as he landed on his feet.

"Well, not as dangerous as some things," he said as his gaze met mine. "Jumping off a roof isn't as dangerous as all the stuff my mother took all those years. Which, now that I think about it, makes it extraordinary that her heart didn't give out a whole lot earlier, you know? Bodes well for me, doesn't it? That I just might live forever with those kinds of genes."

"I... I met her while I was there."

He looked at me, puzzled. "Met who?"

"Your mother."

He didn't say anything for a moment as he stared at me. Then, he managed a curt, "Why?"

Again, I considered the wisdom of telling him any of this. Was I opening up old wounds that Daniel had closed a long time ago? One look at him, at the scared, helpless look in his eyes, even as he scowled at me was confirmation to continue on, though.

"I just... I knew you said she was sick. And that you hadn't been home in a while. I thought it might be helpful if I could –"

"If you could go and see, huh? So, how was it? Was she even cognizant enough to recognize my name?"

My face fell in the light of his anger. "I'm sorry. She was... well, better, I guess than what she must have been like. She wasn't... wasn't using, from what I could tell."

He sneered at me. "Do you even KNOW what it looks like?"

I shook my head.

"She's dangerous, you know," he said. "Well, she *was* dangerous. Manipulative, cold, selfish. I don't like that you went to meet her like that. Even if….you were probably the last person to even see her alive. I would've been worried about *you*, had I known. I couldn't care less about her, but you, Sara? You I actually care about."

I put my hand on his arm, blinking past my tears. "I'm so sorry, Daniel."

"You know," he muttered, exasperated, "I went out to Swakop again, not even two days after everything happened between us. I went out there to tell you that I was wrong, that I didn't mean any of what I said, that I wanted things to be different, for us to −" He stopped and finally met my eyes. "And you were gone. Just gone. With no warning. And it only made me feel that much dumber to have gone out there in the first place, expecting that you meant anything you said."

"But, Daniel," I started, weakly, "I did, and −"

He shook his head, turning around and walking towards the house. When I didn't follow him, he called out, "You stand out here at night, and you're going to get yourself a big heaping helping of malaria, Sara."

I gathered up my bags and followed him into the house. "I don't have to stay here if it… if it won't look right," I managed in a hushed, hurt tone.

"At this time of night it would look worse if you went somewhere else," he said, stepping inside and pulling on a shirt. "And then, I'd just have to worry about you all night. It's easier here. Stay the night. I can sleep on the couch. Or the floor. Or even outside if you're sick of the sight of me."

I stood in the doorway, too emotional to even formulate a response. Try though I might to do otherwise, I couldn't look at him right now without imagining who he had been, going through all he had gone through, so young...

"Ah, geez," he moaned, running his hand through his hair. "I've done it again, right? Said the wrong thing. I'm an idiot, Sara, okay? Is that what you want to hear? I'm just... just always messing things up."

"No," I managed, softly. "It was me, and I –"

"No, no, no, I'm sorry. I just... I've got a whole lot going on. You know? I didn't mean what I said. I just... I'm just having a really crappy week. My mother is dead, the board won't stop trying to call me, and I haven't been able to stop thinking about you since..."

I nodded. "Maybe I should just go back and leave you alone."

"No, it's too late to go back now, and besides... it's good to see you." He looked as though he earnestly and honestly meant it.

I looked up at him hopefully. "Really?"

"Yeah, God help me, really. It's good to see you. Really."

I gave him an uncertain smile.

"Here, let me help you with your stuff," he said, taking my suitcases for me. "Do you want some dinner?"

"Why don't you let me fix dinner for you?," I asked, knowing that I could do this for him at least. "What do we have?" I began going through the cabinets.

"Mielie pap," he said. "That's all. It's been a year since anyone has stayed here. I just came in this morning from Oshakati, and the house there is in great shape. Here, though, the roof is falling apart, I had to kill three snakes in the bathroom, there are bugs everywhere –"

"Even in the mielie pap," I said, showing him.

"Well, great," he said.

"Hey, I have some stuff in my suitcase," I said. "American snacks... is that okay?"

He sat down and looked at me, amused. "Are you in the habit of carrying around American snacks everywhere with you?"

"No, just in my suitcase after I've flown in from the States."

Shock passed over his features. "You just... you just got in today?"

"Seven hours ago... I think. I'm not really sure. It's been a long day."

"And you came to Tsumeb?," he asked, incredulous.

"I was worried about you," I said, struggling to lift my suitcase to the table, moving aside when he took it from my hands to do it for me. "I didn't even know if you were going to be here or not."

"Well, I'm glad I was," he said quietly. "You shouldn't be traveling alone. Not all the way up here."

"I know," I said softly, opening the suitcase which revealed all of my underwear, much to my humiliation.

"Well, there you go," Daniel sighed out unhelpfully, smiling at me in this brief moment of levity.

"Had to replace them, you know," I managed, "since all of my stuff was stolen the last time I flew into Namibia."

"You mean, you haven't been wearing... well, this stuff since you came to Namibia?," he asked, grinning as I blushed.

"No, that's not what I meant. I replaced it all here, of course, but these are –" I stopped and looked at him. "Why am I discussing my underwear with you?"

"I don't know," he said, laughing out loud. "But this is the best discussion I've had in weeks. Maybe months."

"So glad that I could do my part in improving your mood," I muttered. "The snacks are in here," I pushed aside everything else and handed him a box of Goldfish crackers. "See?"

Before long, we had a buffet of American junk food laid out before us... just as the lights flickered out.

"Great," Daniel managed around a mouth full of cupcake. "There's another problem with the Tsumeb house."

"If you'll tell me where the candles are in here, I'll get them," I said, getting up and moving along the furniture to reach the cabinets.

"No, I've got it," he said from very close behind me, causing me to gasp from surprise. "What? Is it another snake?"

"*Snake*?!" I couldn't see anything, and I could feel myself panic. "Daniel, is there a snake in here?!," I gasped again and ran right into his chest, clutching him and trying to get my feet off the ground.

He caught me before I could fall. "Geez, Sara," he whispered, his face close to mine, giving me another reason entirely to gasp. "Scared me half to death."

"Are you scared of snakes?," I whispered, scarcely daring to move now as his arms wound around me, my back pressed against the kitchen counter.

"In the light? No. In the dark? Yeah. You didn't hear one, did you?"

"No."

No matter how many times I blinked, my eyes wouldn't adjust to the darkness. I couldn't see where he was – could only feel his arms around me, his breath so close to my face.

"I just," I managed, breathlessly. "You scared me is all." I leaned forward, now feeling his forehead on mine, our noses just barely touching. I felt him hold his breath, then let it out slowly.

We didn't speak for a long while. We just held each other in the darkness, listening to the sounds outside, which could somehow miraculously be heard over the pounding of my heart.

"I'm sorry about your mother," I whispered.

Silence. Then, softly, "Why did you go see her?"

I thought about the reasons I gave the board, the reasons I told Christy – all about how it was to help Daniel and to relieve some of the burden he was carrying from so far away. But the real reason was one I had kept to myself. Until now. "I wanted to understand why… why you can't trust me."

Again. Silence. "And?"

"I still don't know," I whispered, touching his face with trembling hands.

He kissed the palms of my hands, taking a breath as he did so. "Why'd you come to Tsumeb?"

"I wanted to see you." It wasn't about the board's request, Emmanuel's ignorance, or even about Daniel needing someone to be there for him. It was entirely selfish. I had just wanted to see him.

"I missed you," he said simply. "I always miss you."

"I missed you, too," I said.

"You're so beautiful," he whispered. "Do you know that?"

I let my eyes flutter closed, as he pulled me closer. "You can't even see me," I managed.

"I'm not talking about the way you look," he breathed.

This had been perhaps the first time anyone had said anything like this to me. And the fact that it was coming from him, of all people, made it even more thrilling. "I should have waited to leave until things were more resolved with us—"

"I shouldn't have left Swakopmund without apologizing. Sara, you're seriously the only good thing in my life right now. Honestly."

"Daniel, I think I'm —"

And with that, the lights came back on.

We looked at one another without saying anything for a moment, so much more passing between us as we held one another's gazes. All the frustrations and longings and the misunderstandings and —

"You know, the lights are probably going to go out again soon," he managed. "And you must be tired."

I was more tired than I had let on. "Yeah, I am, actually."

"Why don't you go ahead and take the bedroom and get settled in before the lights go out again?"

I agreed with him, taking just a few necessities from my suitcase as he went to retrieve his own things, then passing him in the small hallway, turning out lights with him as I went.

Ten minutes later, I was in bed, listening to him settle in on the couch as the night sounds outside grew louder and louder.

"Daniel?," I whispered, certain that he would still be able to hear me.

"Yeah?"

"Thanks. For letting me stay."

"No problem." A pause. "Thanks for coming to find me."

I didn't say anything in response.

"I'm sorry about what I said to you at the Bothas' house."

"I'm sorry about what I said at the center," I sighed. "I didn't mean it, you know. About hating any part of this place, and I certainly never meant it about you."

Silence for a moment. Then, "I know."

Just as I was about to begin to ask the questions that had come up since meeting his mother, since diving so deeply into his world stateside, since I had begun thinking about him literally every other moment of every day of my life, he spoke up without any prompting.

"They used to... hit me, you know."

I was surprised by how calmly he said it. "Who hit you?," I asked softly.

Silence. Then, "Her boyfriends. She never stayed with any of them very long. But they were users, too. And they beat the crap out of me when I was little."

I felt my throat tighten up at this, imagining the Daniel of the past and what life must have been like in that little house in Oklahoma. I couldn't stop my tears from falling.

"One of them broke my arm when I was five. She was there when he did it, but she was so far gone that she didn't even try to stop him. She never tried to stop them."

I struggled to keep my voice from breaking. "I'm so sorry, Daniel."

"The longest I ever spent with her at one time was eighteen months. Eighteen months. The rest of the time, my entire childhood, I was being moved from one foster home to another, from one group home to another. And you would think that things would have been better, but they were worse. Always worse. Most of the time I was relieved to be sent back to her because at least then, I knew what I was getting into."

"Did you ever... tell anyone? About all that was happening?," I asked.

"No. I knew, even when I was little, that it wouldn't make a difference. You learn things when you're in the system. And one of them is that complaining will just get you sent somewhere worse." He paused for a long moment. "I did have to testify once, when I was a teenager, about some things that were happening at a group home. I swear to you, sometimes if I let myself think about it, about any of that time, I feel like I could go back and kill them all with my bare hands."

My head was pounding with this confirmation of all that I had heard. How Daniel was making so much more sense to me now, how it was worse than I could have imagined, how –

"You know," he said, thoughtfully, "I'd be just as bad as all of them. Worse probably, if God hadn't changed my life. I know who I would have been without Him. Because I see who they were, who she was. And I know who I am, and I'm not all that different, really."

I thought over my words carefully, not wanting to scare him away, yet wanting him to say more, to share more, and to finally let me in. "You're not bound by what they did. By any of it. You aren't like them."

"But I'm just as messed up," he said. "I mean, here I am, saying that Christ has changed my life completely and that I'm dead to the past and all that happened to me. Yet the first real opportunity I have to love someone, to be loved by someone, what do I do? I send her running away as fast as she can go."

"I came back," I whispered.

He didn't say anything for a moment. "You know, all of the times I tried to help my mother, after I was grown and supposedly 'healed' from all the hurt, I couldn't understand why she kept throwing away the chance to make things right. How she kept taking my trust and destroying it, again and again. And I've been killing myself thinking that you're going to be just like her one day, taking any trust I put in you and showing me to be some huge fool for believing that you could really care about me." A pause, then softly, "But the more I think about it, the more I'm convinced that you're not just like her. *I'm* just like her. And I'm hurting you worse than she ever hurt me."

Every part of me wanted to run to the living room and be with him, to tell him that he was wrong and to move past all of this. But I stayed where I was, wiped my nose with the back of my hand, and managed simply these words. "Daniel, she... she loved you. Even if she couldn't be who you needed her to be."

"No," he said, resigned. "I don't think she had it in her to love anyone. I don't think I do either most of the time."

And then, there was nothing else. Only silence. And the sounds that continued on outside the lonely little house in Tsumeb.

I woke up the next morning, confused as to where I was. Slowly, my mind turned to the evening before, to all of Daniel's confessions through the dark house, and I remembered every moment. I could hear him moving in the kitchen, the scent of bacon and eggs accompanying what he was doing, and my stomach growled in response.

I was starving, but I was surprisingly refreshed after what felt like a long night's sleep. Taking stock of the tiny bedroom in the Tsumeb house, I hurried to the bathroom to finally get cleaned up as quickly as I could.

He was in the kitchen, standing at the stove when I finally made it in there. He looked over his shoulder at me, then looked back at the food he was cooking, a self-conscious smile on his face. "So, you finally decided to wake up?"

"That sounds familiar, you know," I managed, watching him from the doorway.

"I imagine, it does," he said. "But you never slept so late when we were camping." He looked at me, a small smile playing on his lips. "Nice shirt."

I pulled it close to me. "It's yours."

"I remember," he said. "You never gave it back to me after that night in the Himba village."

"I could give it to you now," I said, blushing at the unintended implication that I would just strip right down in the kitchen. He raised his eyebrows at this, smiling again, and shook his head.

"No, I like that you kept it."

I moved over to stand next to him at the stove, surprised and flustered when he leaned over and kissed my cheek.

"You smell good," he whispered.

"Thanks," I whispered back. "Good rest and a shower."

"Well, you certainly did get some good rest," he confirmed. "Slept half the day, actually."

"How late is it..." I glanced to the clock on the kitchen wall and gasped. "I've been asleep for... eighteen hours!"

He shrugged. "I don't know how that's even possible, since jet lag usually has people waking up in the middle of the night. I peeked in on you a couple of times to make sure you were still alive, and you were snoring."

I hit his shoulder. "I don't snore."

"Mmmhmm," he grinned. "Anyway, you should be back to your normal

Namibian schedule in a couple of days if last night's sleep was any indication."

"No wonder I'm starving," I said, linking my arm through his and leaning against his shoulder. Oh, he felt so good. "Where was all of this food last night?"

"At the store still," he said softly. "Tsumeb doesn't have much, but it does have bacon and eggs."

"Praise God," I yawned. "Hey, I have something that might go with this."

I went to my suitcases and pulled out a bottle of homemade salsa and a package of tortillas. I presented them to him with a flourish.

"Where was that?," he asked.

"In my luggage."

He smiled at me. "How much food did you bring?"

"Not much else. Just what I knew I wouldn't be able to find here."

"You should keep it instead of using it all up tonight," he said.

"Rather eat it with you than by myself, honestly."

I looked at him, thinking on our conversation from the night before, wondering what he was thinking, if we would revisit any of the details, or if –

"Well, it's about ready anyway," he said, planting a small kiss on my lips before transferring the food to two plates.

Breakfast, or whatever this strange meal was, given the odd hour at which we ate it, was quiet. I'd look up from my plate to find Daniel watching me and start to ask him a question about our conversation the night before, only to have him fill me in on mission business that I had missed while I was gone.

"And then," he concluded, after a long story about the trip to Luderitz with Willem last week, "we went back up to Swakopmund. They finally finished getting the security system in place. Riaan knows all the codes and will get you updated on the details once we get you back there."

"We can't go back now, can we?," I said, meaning several different things with my one statement. Couldn't go back to Swakop this late, couldn't go back to what we had been before the night at the Strand, couldn't go back to how it was when I didn't know half of what I now knew about him...

Daniel watched me for a moment, considering the truth of this. He focused on the most pressing issue at the moment, though, which was leaving Tsumeb. "No, likely not. We'll have to leave tomorrow morning."

"I'm sorry to have slept so late," I sighed. "You should have woken me up. Then you wouldn't be... stuck here."

"I needed to get some things done to the house anyway," he said. Then, watching me, "And it's no great hardship, Sara, being stuck here with you."

I finished the last bite on my plate, considering this. "Have you spoken with the board?"

"Nope," he said, shaking his head. "Emmanuel called to tell me about my mother, but... I haven't returned the board's calls."

I swallowed, weighing my words carefully. "I think... that they probably know more about you now than they did. And it's likely my fault, for getting them back in touch with your mother."

He put his arms on the table and leaned forward. "I didn't hide any of it from them," he said, calmly. "But they'll probably want to speak with me, to… you know, make sure I'm well adjusted and all. Whatever that means, right?"

"Shame, Daniel," I murmured, reaching over and touching his hand.

He smiled at this. "And here they only thought they were dealing with a crazy pioneer missionary in the wilds of Africa. I just got ten times more interesting, didn't I?"

"You were plenty interesting enough already," I said. "I'm sure they just… just want to make sure you're okay."

"Yeah."

After a moment of silence, I took a deep breath. "I'll clean up the dishes," I said, softly, stopping his protests with my hand. "Seriously, you cooked it all, so I'll take care of this."

I cleared the table, ran the water for the dishes, and looked out the window over the sink, noting that already the sun was nearing the horizon. The sunset was less than an hour away, and I was completely awake. It was going to be a long, long night.

I sighed at the thought of this, wondering through so many of the unspoken issues  about what came next still lingering between Daniel and me, washing dishes as I thought about what I should say, what I should do, what I should –

And even as I ran through the options in my mind, I could feel Daniel move behind me, softly put his arms around my waist, and rest his chin on my shoulder. I closed my eyes at his close proximity and sighed again.

Oh, who even cared that I had no answers at this point. This, Daniel right here with me, so close to me right now, was all the answer I really cared to have anyway.

I turned to face him, putting my arms around him, not even bothering to dry my hands off as I did so.

"Shame, man," I whispered, "I'm getting you all wet."

He leaned his forehead against mine. "That is, very seriously, the last concern I have at this point."

We stared at one another for a long moment, neither of us saying anything. Then, he softly said, "Tell me something about your family."

I closed my eyes for a second, thinking and wondering over this. "Well," I began, looking back at him, "my dad's a dentist. My mom runs the accounting end of his practice. We have a miniature dachshund named Ginger."

"Ginger," he said.

"Yes," I breathed, still wondering at his closeness and where this conversation was going. "Were dog names not what you had in mind when you asked about my family?"

"Well, no, that's fine," he said, then sighed. "I guess I'm just trying to get a picture of what it was like for you. You know, growing up in your normal family."

I thought about this for a second. "Just normal. And boring probably."

"Probably not," he said. "Tell me about... the best vacation you took. As a family. That's something normal families do, right? Take vacations together?"

"Yeah," I said, smiling at one particular memory. "Walt Disney World. When I was six."

"I'll bet you were a really cute six year old," he smiled at me.

"I was," I sighed, smiling at this. "Anyway, we were in the Magic Kingdom, which for a six year old girl who thinks she's a princess is the equivalent of every fantasy ever conceived being brought to life."

"Did you dress up?"

"As a matter of fact, I did," I said. "Cinderella. Mistreated by her rotten family until the…" I cut my statement short, my mind running over his history.

"It's okay," he said softly.

"Well, anyway," I began again, "there we were just getting off of Dumbo, with me in my giant princess dress, right by the big castle. And I decided that I needed an ice cream bar."

"An ice cream bar? Shaped like Mickey Mouse?"

I smiled at him. "Actually, yes. How did you know that?"

"It was just a guess," he said, brushing his lips against mine, causing my breath to catch in my throat. "Honestly, they make such a thing?"

"Oh, yeah, and it's delicious," I said, still staring at his lips.

"And…?," he prompted, clearly amused.

"And I pitched a huge fit when my mother said it was too close to dinner," I said. "Here they had paid all this money for this vacation, had spent all day riding these rides that were brain-numbing for adults, had gone and gotten me this fabulous princess dress, and I threw myself on the pavement right by the castle and pitched the biggest fit of my life." I smiled at him. "Isn't that a happy story?"

"Did your parents beat the crap out of you for that little stunt?," Daniel smiled as he said it.

"Well… no. Of course not." My eyes filled with tears at the memory, at the fact that Daniel's assumptions would naturally be so very different from my own reality. "My dad picked me up, wiped my tears away, and distracted me by taking me on another ride. And after dinner? I got that ice cream. Even though I didn't deserve it. And I fell asleep on the way back to the hotel, still in that princess dress, which was completely covered in ice cream stains."

He thought about this for a moment. "I would've gotten you ice cream, too." He smiled at me. "As bad as my own childhood was, I'd still buy my own children ice cream like that, even if they didn't deserve it. I can promise you that."

"You're going to be a great dad, Daniel," I said, kissing him again, longer this time.

"I'm so glad you came to Tsumeb," he whispered.

"If this is what Tsumeb is always like, I may never leave," I whispered back to him.

A small laugh, another kiss, and then a sigh. "I loved your story. Your story about your perfectly normal family vacation."

"I guess it was," I whispered. "Daniel, are you okay?"

He looked at me for a moment, considering his words. "Yeah, my turn now." He took a deep breath. "When I was fourteen, the state sent me to live at another foster home... with the Burkes, an older couple who had no idea what they were getting into with me. I was out of the group home, which was good. And the trial was over, and the state told me it would all be better for me now, but I had been in enough foster homes with families to know that... well, that they weren't much better than living with my mother and her boyfriends. But this couple? The Burkes? They were different. And I gave them such a hard time. I mean, I was a living terror while I was with them. I'm sure everyone told them I needed psychiatric help, and they were likely right to tell them that. But they were so patient, even as I physically destroyed parts of their home, yelled the worst things at them, and kept getting into trouble at school and at the church they went to." He paused for a moment. "They took me on vacation the summer I was with them. To

Graceland."

I grimaced. "Oh, no…"

"Oh, yeah," he laughed. "They were big Elvis fans, and they honestly believed that Graceland was the dream destination of your typical fourteen year old boy. They loaded up the car, and we drove all the way out to Tennessee. And I thought I got to know them while living in their house, but that vacation? Well, I saw how they really were. And no matter what I did to them, no matter how rotten I was during the days of that vacation, do you know what they did? Every night?"

I shook my head, scarcely daring to breathe and fracture this moment.

"They prayed for me. Prayed over me. They had no idea what I had gone through and were at a total loss as to what to do with me. But they prayed for me. And I despised it. And I despised them. Until God began changing my heart. Fractionally at first, then more and more as they lived for Christ right before me. And the word of God… changed everything. And as I read it, He changed me. But by then? Well, the state had moved me back with my mother because she was supposedly clean again, and with the press of the trial dying down and their inability to even decide what to do with me then… well, whatever. Nothing had changed. It was more of the same. But I had changed. And I was nearly grown. It made a difference. Christ made a difference. And I survived."

"Did you ever go back? To the Burke family? To tell them what had happened?"

He shook his head. "Just sent them a note when I finished seminary, thanking them, but I never left a return address."

"Wow, Daniel," I said, drawing him closer to me, "what a blessing to them, to know that they played any part in making you the man you are today."

"And what man is that?," he asked, looking at me doubtfully.

"A man who has given his entire life to ministry in a difficult place," I murmured. "Who is passionate about God's Word, has a heart for people who are hurting, and who is making a difference with the redemption he's been given."

He watched me for a moment. "Why did I tell you all of these things?," he asked softly. "I swear, Sara, I've never told anyone *any* of these things."

I felt the tears gathering in my eyes. "I don't know," I said softly. "But I'm glad you did."

"You know, I've always thought that life would be a whole lot easier for me if I could just run away up north without anyone to deal with, except the people I'm sharing with along the way," he said. "And then? I met you, and it's the craziest, dumbest thing ever, but now, I'm spending all this time thinking that kind of life would be crappy because you wouldn't be with me."

I leaned forward and kissed him, not bothering to wipe away the tears that had started rolling down my cheeks. It wasn't the passionate, harried kiss that we had shared on the Strand, but this one was even more intense, all while being gentle, sincere, and so heartbreakingly sweet.

"Sara," he said, as he continued to hold me, "I want nothing more than to never leave this house and just completely escape everything waiting for me in the real world."

"Hey," I whispered, touching his face, causing him to look at me. "We don't have to go back to reality until tomorrow."

And I let him lead me to the living room, where one heartfelt, agonizingly devoted kiss multiplied into countless others, as we continued softly talking, holding one another close, and trying our best to forget reality, even as the sun came up outside.

He drove me back to Swakopmund the next day.

There was no talk of his mother, of our conversation the night before, of any of it. He was the Daniel of the year before, but gentler now, pointing out things to me as we drove to the coast, going over plans for my work as Namibia flew by us.

Once we arrived at my flat, I looked to him curiously. "Are you okay?," I asked.

He nodded, offering me a smile. "I'm fine."

"Do you want to come in? You haven't had anything to eat all day. I can fix something, and –"

He shook his head. "I actually should get back to Windhoek. Call the board, make some arrangements to get that roof fixed in Tsumeb, make sure Emmanuel hasn't spent all the petty cash at the shebeen. You know, things like that."

"Are you sure?," I asked, worried by all that he wasn't saying.

"I'm sure," he said softly. Then, he leaned over and kissed me gently. "Can you trust me, Sara?"

"I already do," I murmured.

He gave me one last smile in response.

And then, he was gone.

# 10 CHAPTER TEN

I have a sense for big moments.

I get that feeling, of dread, of anticipation, a precursor to the big moments in life that are about to unfold before me.

And I got it again two days later when Emmanuel called me, bright and early.

"Princess!," he exclaimed when I answered the phone. "I was hoping to catch you before you went out for the day!"

"You caught me just in time, friend," I said. "Big plans for the center today. And preparations for the next few weeks in the DRC with the men's ministry as well." Then tentatively, as I hadn't heard from him myself, "I don't suppose Brother Daniel has given you any idea when he plans on coming out to Swakop to assist, huh?"

"Had he made plans to assist, Princess?," Emmanuel asked, confused.

"I had hoped," I sighed. "Perhaps he's spoken to Willem about it all."

"I don't think he will be assisting any time soon," Emmanuel said. "Which is the whole reason I am calling you, Sara."

"What's going on?"

"Well, I am hopeful that *you* will come to Windhoek soon," he said.

Had Daniel asked for me to come out? Had he made mention to Emmanuel that he wanted me there? Before I could think of how to phrase the questions that were running through my mind, so as to not give Emmanuel the wrong idea, he said the words that washed me in cold dread.

"I need a member of the board to authorize some documents, and with Brother Daniel having left Namibia, you are the only one to do it."

My heart froze in my chest. "Emmanuel, what are you talking about? Where has Brother Daniel gone?"

He clicked his tongue at me from hundreds of miles away in the capitol city. "Princess, he has gone back to the United States. He has taken another position with the board." A pause. "Did you not know?"

It wasn't hard to figure out what had happened. And after a few phone calls to the right offices at the board stateside, I knew what Daniel had done once he got to Windhoek.

He had asked for a leave of absence, a sabbatical, to get things in order after his mother's death. There wasn't much to be done in reality, but I knew that emotionally, there was so much for him to work through and that he hadn't been able to even realize the half of it as he ran things in Namibia. It had been a good distraction for him all these years, but these past few months... he had been forced to ask some tough questions. And he stopped avoiding the past.

It all was public record. Or most of it anyway. What Daniel had gone through in the system, what he had been forced to testify about before he even honestly came of age, and what he had been dealing with for so many years. I hadn't known. His mother had alluded to so much that I hadn't known, and I would never have imagined, in all the horrific scenarios I could have imagined in my darkest nightmares, what Daniel had gone through. It was a miracle that he wasn't more wounded than he was and it was nothing short of the transformation of Christ that explained how he was able to be who he was, even with all that still haunted him.

I made many phone calls that afternoon, then sat on the floor of my flat, my back against the wall, my cell phone held close to my chest, as silent tears ran down my face, each one a prayer, asking for wisdom to know what to do. I had learned that one of the conditions of Daniel's sabbatical had been that he would do some work stateside for the board, recruiting for the southern Africa team at the conventions, the larger churches, and the seminaries. I couldn't think of a worse recruiter than intense, brooding Daniel, but he had agreed to it. He was in Oklahoma right now, on personal business, and was scheduled to go to Texas soon. He would be at the seminary in Fort Worth for two months.

And while my head told me that it was insane to follow a man who had so much to sort out on his own without any more complications from me, that it was a supremely dumb idea oh so typical of me to follow a man who had made no promises for any kind of future, I couldn't stop myself from making arrangements to be there to meet him, to try to work through this all beside him, where I knew I belonged.

The work would continue on without me, and in the hands of those who understood so many things so much better than I had, despite my best intentions and efforts, it would do well.

"Everything has an end. Except for sausage. It has two," Willem said to me, with no small amount of falsified wisdom, as we all said goodbye.

"Well... thank you for that. I'm not sure... what it even means."

He shrugged. "Me neither. It's a German thing, I think." He smiled his crooked smile at me and hugged me one last time.

"We will miss you," Ana Marie pushed her brother aside and held me close as she cried, as Riaan continued to unload my bags from the boot of the car. "Will you come back and visit us?" Her tears were for the goodbyes, of course, but were certainly helped along by the pregnancy, the news of which had been a wonderful surprise to us all that last week. I felt the tears roll down my cheeks as I thought of leaving and never seeing her and her growing family again.

"I will do my best, friend," I told her.

"You tell Daniel to get his rubbish together and *get back here*. And bring you with him!," Riaan said, hugging me as well.

They didn't know the half of Daniel's rubbish, but they knew enough to know that my journey had more to do with him than it did with leaving Namibia. I smiled at all three of them, looking around one last time at Namibia before entering the airport and saying my goodbyes...

... for now.


To: Sara Wright (sarawright@gonowmissions.org)

From: Daniel Boyd (danielboyd@gonowmissions.org)

Subject:

Sara, I've been trying to call you for the past two days. I wanted to explain why I left without telling you anything. But you're not answering your phone.

Please let me know that you're okay, even if you don't want to speak to me anymore.

Please.

Daniel

Only two days back in the US, and I had finished up all of my hire paperwork at the school, making arrangements to fill in for another kindergarten teacher in the district who would be on maternity leave soon. It wouldn't be the salary I had made before I went overseas, but it would be enough to live on as I waited on what God had next.

My drive back to my parents' house led me right by the seminary. I already knew that he would be there, in an office at the back of the missions building, and without any hesitation at all, I made my way there, not stopping until I was standing at his open door.

He was on the phone, just as he had been the first time I saw him in Windhoek. And just as he had been that first afternoon, he was clearly irritated with whomever he was speaking to, as evidenced by his furrowed forehead and clenched fist on the desk. But when his eyes met mine, his expression held no malice or frustration. Only wonder.

That was different.

He said a quick, albeit menacing, goodbye to the person on the other end of the phone, then looked back at me. "Sara? What are you doing here?"

I couldn't stop from smiling as I went to sit across from him. "I was in the neighborhood."

He looked at me incredulously for a moment. "From Swakopmund to here?" And imitating Emmanuel's voice, "This is one big neighborhood."

"That it is," I laughed, then feeling the tears in my eyes, softly said, "You never told me you were leaving."

He sighed, a pained expression on his face. "No, I didn't."

We sat in silence for a moment. Then, he attempted to explain himself. "It was stupid. Leaving like that. But, Sara, I wanted to see you too much."

This wasn't much of an explanation. But I understood what he meant.

"I got your email. And your missed calls," I said. "I was on the plane... well, the planes, while you were sending them and making them."

"Then you know that I tried to get in touch with you, just as soon as I could, and—"

"I didn't help things in Tsumeb, did I? Not when I came in expecting so much."

He shook his head. "No, you *did* help. You were exactly who I needed. You heard some things I've needed to say for a long time. And you let me... you let me see what it could really be like if I could finally move past everything. You're the only reason I wanted to try. After I went to Windhoek, I was going to come back to Swakop to tell you that I had resigned my position for a leave of absence. There were some things here, stateside, that I... well, that I needed to work on."

I nodded my head.

"But I..." He looked down at his hands for a moment. Then, his eyes found mine again. "I didn't make it, though. I wanted to go and tell you, but I was afraid that I wouldn't leave if I saw you and... you said you would trust me. And I knew I had to get right, had to get past all of this crap, to make things right. I didn't want to keep putting us both through this. I didn't want to complicate things any more than they already were."

"Daniel," I said softly, "I think I'm figuring out that life with you? Is going to be complicated."

He allowed himself a small smile. "To put it mildly... yeah, probably so. But... it's getting better. I've been back to Oklahoma. I saw the Burkes."

"Did you?," I asked, sitting up in my chair. "Were they…"

"They weren't surprised to see me," he said, smiling. "Which was weird, of course. But they said they'd been praying, all these years. And… well, they were just as wonderful as they had always been."

"Daniel, I'm so happy for you. Really."

"I told them," he said, looking up at me with such honest vulnerability in his eyes, "about you. About how I wanted to bring you back to meet them one day."

I sighed. "I would love that."

He bit his lip thoughtfully. "Are you here in the US for a while? When do you head back?"

"I've resigned as well," I said. "I'm here until… well, until God tells me to move on."

He looked concerned. "But the center, the work with the ladies –"

"All still will go on, without me. Riaan and Ana Marie, and even Willem, have taken it over. And they have bigger plans than I had in the DRC. Seem to understand it better than I did, as someone suggested that nationals might."

"Must have been some arrogant fool who said that," he managed.

"Yes, but he was right."

"And now, you've worked yourself out of a job," he smiled, "on the advice of that same arrogant fool, I would imagine."

"Pretty much. Working myself out of a job -- wasn't that the goal?"

"Was it?"

I sighed heavily. "I don't know, Daniel. I'm still trying to figure out what the whole point was of... well, of everything."

"You were wonderful there. Just right where you were supposed to be."

I nodded. "And now..." I looked at him. "I'm right where I need to be again."

We sat in silence for a moment. Then, Daniel was on his feet, pulling me out of my chair, and into his arms. I could feel his shoulders relax as he let out a relieved breath. We stood together, holding on tightly to one another, not saying anything for a long moment.

"I love you," he finally whispered.

I closed my eyes just as the first tears began to fall.

He wasn't done, though. "I'm going to be someone you can trust."

"We're going to figure this out together," I said.

He held me tighter. "I shouldn't have left without making sure you knew. And I can tell you that I would've gone back to get you, to make things right, but I was such a mess that I don't know if I –"

"You don't need to worry about that now, because I'm here with you."

"I want you to be with me," he said, holding my face in his hands. "To just finally be with me, all of my crap and baggage and... I don't want to go anywhere without you."

I sighed. "Okay."

He smiled at me, a smile like one of those rare ones I had seen during the good times in Namibia. "Okay? Just like that?"

"Yeah, just like that," I said. "I had a really, really long flight over here to think about it."

He allowed himself a small laugh. Then, he leaned his forehead on mine again, taking a deep breath. "I don't deserve another chance. I know that. I can't believe you're going to just be okay with... with all of this."

"You're not perfect," I said, softly. "And this? You and me? Probably won't be perfect. And I think knowing that from the beginning? Probably puts us in a better place than most, right?"

"Absolutely," he smiled, kissing me. Oh, I had missed this. "I'm glad you had that long flight to think through this."

"Well, the eighteen hours of sleep afterwards helped, too," I smiled up at him.

"Amazing, again," he said. "I'm still not over the jet lag. And speaking of long flights, I've been making arrangements for Mr. Shiftoka to finally – *finally* – be on his way to Windhoek in the fall."

I looked up at him, our arms still around one another. "Ahh, shame, man. Mr. Shiftoka will be able to do all the impossible things the American princess could not, right?"

"Will I ever live any of that down?," Daniel pressed his forehead against mine, so many unspoken apologies and entreaties in his eyes.

"Maybe," I whispered. "But it's probably going to take the next fifty years or so."

"I can live with that," he whispered before kissing me again.


We had been together in the US for two weeks. Two amazing, incredible, world changing weeks.

In Namibia, he had been slow to trust me, hard to communicate with, and so difficult to understand. After I came back to the US, though, he completely changed. For as much as he held back before, he was now completely and totally here with me. Nothing was left unsaid, nothing was taken for granted, and nothing was up for doubts when it came to how he felt about me and what lengths he would go to in order for us to stay together. To the degree that he had been aloof and standoffish at the beginning, he was now devoted and engaged.

And that? Probably looked a little intense to everyone else. Especially on Daniel, who had always been intense anyway.

Emily and Melissa had been insistent on meeting him, now that we were all in the same place again, and we had all met up, along with Josh and Beau, for dinner. All three men clicked easily and naturally, but Mel and Em kept quiet for most of the dinner, shooting glances at me, at Daniel, and at one another. I had wondered at this, about their concern, but there in the ladies' room, their thoughts were made crystal clear.

"He's a little... intense." Melissa gave me a concerned look from where we stood washing our hands.

"I know," I said, smiling at her.

"Well, intense," Emily said, her hand resting on forty week plus baby bump. "That's a word for it." She smiled at me. "But I think it looks more like... well, like he's ready to die for you or something. Just... so serious and..."

"Intense," Melissa said.

"Well," Emily said, nodding. "Yeah."

"He's not going anywhere, is he?," Melissa said. "I mean, not without you."

I shook my head. "I don't think so. And that's fine by me."

"Oh, Sara," Emily smiled, pulling me close and hugging me. "I'm so happy for you, and – oh, crap!"

"What?," Mel asked, glancing over from where she was drying her hands.

"I just wet my pants," Em whispered fiercely. "This pregnancy has made it impossible to retain *any* control of my bladder!"

"Ew." Melissa gave her a look.

"Yeah, tell me about it," Emily muttered. "All these years and all the horror stories my sister has told me about pregnancy, and she *never* said anything about *this*."

"Do you… regularly do this?," I asked, as she tried to check out the damage in the mirror.

"No, thankfully," she said. "Just one other time about a week ago when Josh, and I quote, 'took his preggo for a walk' and made me start laughing, and I –" She suddenly gasped. "*Whoa*."

"Geez, are you peeing again?," Mel asked.

"No," Emily said softly. "I think I just… had a contraction."

I gasped at this, while Melissa frowned. "Are you sure it's not just indigestion? Because you were really putting the chow away out there, and –"

"Oh, trust me," Emily managed. "This pain is coming from a place where indigestion doesn't dare venture, and…" She looked up at me, surprise in her eyes. "That wasn't pee! My water broke!"

I smiled, reaching out to touch her bump, cooing through more tears as I did so. "Oh, sweet baby Sadie, thank you for waiting for Aunt Sara to come home for your birthday!"

Emily laughed out loud, as Mel rushed over to her. "Are you sure? Maybe it's just –"

"Oh, no," Emily assured her. "This is it. Finally!"

"Come on, Mama," I said, pulling her along, grinning. "Let's go tell Papi Josh it's time to get to the hospital and meet that sweet baby girl!"

Six months later, the board told Daniel to go back to Namibia.

He had been working through many things, we had been working through them together, and he felt it was time. The board had allowed him to stay on in Fort Worth, recruiting and speaking all over Texas for half a year, taking into consideration, at last, all that he was going through with his counseling, with our counseling, with the peace he was finally making with the past. And now, they were asking him to go back home.

"Marry me," he said on the night we got word about the board's plans. "I can call them right now, tell them to make arrangements for us both."

"You have to leave next week, though," I said to him, weak at the prospect of watching him leave, my mind hardly touching on his proposal.

He looked at me as if he didn't understand what the problem was. "And?"

"Daniel, that's only seven days to change our entire lives, and –"

But I stopped myself. What was it really changing anyway? We had spent these months working towards something, working towards it together, and being together from now on? Was a foregone conclusion. I could see it in his eyes, had seen it there from the moment I met him back in the US, and now? Now it was reality.

So really? There was no problem. Especially if the alternative to taking more time was letting him go back alone.

"Okay," I said. "I will."

I had made Emily promise, years earlier, to be my wedding coordinator. And on the afternoon that Daniel and I came back to my parents' house after picking up rings and a marriage license, I called to cash in on her promise. She was ecstatic at the news of my engagement... and panicked when I told her that we had less than a week until the wedding.

Our engagement and all the preparations were, as everything had been between Daniel and me, unconventional. He was with me when I picked out a wedding dress, with me when I made the few decisions that had to be made for the small ceremony, and with me when I began packing up our combined four suitcases.

He was with me. All the time. And there was great comfort in pausing whatever we were doing, holding onto one another, and celebrating, that from now on, there would be no more lonely days or lonely nights in Namibia because we would be together.

The wedding was perfect.

Nothing like what I had imagined in my little girl dreams, of course... but certainly more than fitting for the woman I had become.

My parents stood as witnesses, along with the Burkes, Beau, Melissa, and Emily, as Josh led us through our vows.

Promises made with rings and smiles, about here and now, and healing from the past, and expectations for an uncertain future, where the certainty was being together, wherever God sent us. The intensity with which we made the promises made them all the more believable, as we clutched one another's hands tightly, our attention completely on one another, almost forgetting that anyone else was there.

It was quick. But it had to be out of necessity, since we had to leave so soon. There had been no time until now to gather everyone together, so we had wanted to wait for this moment, where those we loved best could be here to witness the covenant we made as one in Christ, sealing it with a long, lingering kiss full of promise for a lifetime together half a world away.

There was cake. Quickly shared and enjoyed. And prayers prayed and words spoken over us, simply and joyfully, as we watched the clock until there was no time left. Daniel leaned over to kiss my forehead softly, wordlessly communicating that it was time to go.

"This is so weird," Melissa had muttered to me as she hugged her congratulations. "No big party or anything. Totally not what I ever predicted we'd be doing for you."

"Not enough time," I smiled at her. "Flight leaves in just a few hours."

"Quickest wedding I've ever done," Josh smiled, signing the license and shaking Daniel's hand one last time. "I'll send it in, and Emily –"

"Will get you the list of everything you need to legally change your name to Sara Boyd while you're in Namibia," she said, hugging me. Then, she burst into tears.

"Ah, geez," Melissa rolled her eyes.

"I'm sorry," Emily managed in between gasps. "I'm just a big, hormonal, pregnant mess. Again." Little Sadie was only six months old, but Emily was already three months along. Our next trip to the US would have us visiting two tiny Morales children. Or more if we tarried too long.

There were certainly very good days ahead for us. For all of us.


All those flights later, we were finally in a taxi heading towards the center of Windhoek, where my new husband held me close, encouraging me to rest while he gave directions to the driver in the

Oshiwambo that he hadn't lost in the six months we'd been gone, leading us home at last.

After the goodbyes, my parents had taken us to the airport with our four pieces of luggage. They had sworn that it was even more difficult now, as they weren't just sending a daughter but a son as well, as Daniel had become very dear to them in the six months they'd been able to know him. We had made plans for them to come and visit soon.

Many more tears later, tears that felt heavy with finality, we were half a world away. Just the two of us.

"You okay?," Daniel whispered, as I napped on his shoulder.

"Yeah... I'm exhausted."

"You'll be fine after eighteen hours of sleep," he said, smiling at me.

"I'm looking forward to every minute," I said, snuggling in closer to him. "Are we almost there?"

Windhoek flew by us in snatches and snippets, everything blurring together in the dark of night. "Almost," he murmured.

"It's so hot outside," I said, wiping the sweat from my forehead.

"East wind," he smiled. "Just like the last time you flew into Windhoek, remember?"

"Hmm..." I grinned. "You're considerably less grumpy this time around."

"I have more to look forward to," he whispered in my ear.

Before long, the gates of the mission came into view. With a quick kiss to my forehead, Daniel got out, opened up the gate with the key he still carried, and motioned our driver inside. We unpacked the car, waved him on, and approached our home together.

"Emmanuel texted me that he would be back tomorrow morning,"

Daniel said, sweeping me up into his arms as we crossed the threshold.

"How chivalrous," I smiled at him.

"Not really," Daniel grinned. "It is his job after all."

"You, not Emmanuel."

"Oh," he stretched his arms over his head, relaxing after so many long flights. Then, he smiled at me. "He'll be good and surprised to find you here with me tomorrow, though."

"You didn't tell him I was coming?"

"Didn't tell him a thing. Not that you're here, not that we're married, none of it." He smiled. "I want to see how long it takes him to start asking some questions about the impropriety of you being in my bed all night."

"Something I've been looking forward to for a long, long, time, Daniel," I put my arms around him, fighting back a yawn as I smiled up at him.

"Me, too," he said softly, leaning down to kiss me, then taking my hand. "Come on. I made a promise to you once that I intend to keep now."

And he led me outside, turning off all the exterior lights on the property as he did so, until we were plunged into complete darkness. He wrapped his arms around my waist, pulled me back into his chest, and directed my chin up to see... the stars. Countless, infinite, different stars, in constellations that were...

"Ours," Daniel whispered. "Mine and yours."

"Beautiful," I whispered back.

"Welcome home, Sara."

*BEST DAY EVER...*
*COMING OUT SEPTEMBER 2013!*

Chloe Thibideaux is running out of options. College didn't work out. Her parents took away all of her credit cards. And her social life? Yeah, that fell completely apart through no fault of her own. Homeless, alone, and in serious need of some retail therapy, she's forced to beg her brother, Beau, and his wife, Melissa, to let her stay with them until she can figure out what she's going to do with the rest of her life.

As she discovers abilities, talents, and dreams she never knew she had before, she begins to learn about who she is and who she can be in Christ. With the help of her new community of friends, which includes the "smokin' hot" Pastor Stephen, Chloe is becoming someone completely new... but will her past keep her from all that God has in store for her?